T0380674

NO BOUNDARIES

...but mom, I love him!

RacQuel Gemini

Copyright © 2023 RacQuel Gemini.

All rights reserved. No part of this book may be used or reproduced by any means, graphic, electronic, or mechanical, including photocopying, recording, taping or by any information storage retrieval system without the written permission of the author except in the case of brief quotations embodied in critical articles and reviews.

This is a work of fiction. All of the characters, names, incidents, organizations, and dialogue in this novel are either the products of the author's imagination or are used fictitiously.

Archway Publishing books may be ordered through booksellers or by contacting:

Archway Publishing
1663 Liberty Drive
Bloomington, IN 47403
www.archwaypublishing.com
844-669-3957

Because of the dynamic nature of the Internet, any web addresses or links contained in this book may have changed since publication and may no longer be valid. The views expressed in this work are solely those of the author and do not necessarily reflect the views of the publisher, and the publisher hereby disclaims any responsibility for them.

Any people depicted in stock imagery provided by Getty Images are models, and such images are being used for illustrative purposes only.
Certain stock imagery © Getty Images.

ISBN: 978-1-6657-4745-5 (sc)
ISBN: 978-1-6657-4746-2 (e)

Library of Congress Control Number: 2023913696

Print information available on the last page.

Archway Publishing rev. date: 07/31/2023

PROLOGUE

"I can't do this anymore. I'm leaving and nothing you say or do is going to change my mind!"

The shout echoes in the small house but seven years old, Starr Dixon doesn't even flinch at the words.

She doesn't even look in the direction of the sound. She looks unaffected but she is anything but.

Her young eyes are dry but inside, she is crying. She had learned that the physical tears brought her nothing but a headache so what use are they?

She is seating at a bay window that faces the street of the tiny home where she, her mother and father live. In her peripheral, she can see the two grownups while people outside go about their business, oblivious to the troubles just a short distance away. Mom and Dad's hand gestures are sharp, their body motions are defensive and their words are loud. Their words are hurtful, not only to each other but to their child.

It is not the first time that Starr is witnessing her father, Travis, and mother, Mary having an argument. In fact, lately, that is all they seem to do.

It was not always like this. Although her mind is young, Starr remembers a time when Travis and Mary were always laughing and touching lovingly. Their easy relationship had filled the home with warmth and made her feel safe and secure.

She doesn't know why but things have changed now and the small home that was once overflowing with laughter and joy always carried a distressed undertone even when the two adults are not quarreling. They would seemingly forget she was around and say the bad words they told her not to repeat.

That is why she is seating off to the side like a good little girl with her legs folded beneath her pink polka dot dress with her hands neatly rested on her legs. She cannot help thinking that if she is good enough, they would stop being so loud and hurtful to each other.

Besides, when she sat quietly like this and looked outside, she could pretend her current reality is not real.

Her mind would wander and replay the stories she likes to read with her mom and dad at bedtime. She dreams of the happy characters in those books when she sleeps often and cannot help but hope that maybe this is all just a bad dream and she will wake up soon to the home she knew before that was filled with happiness and love.

"You cannot do this, Travis. You cannot leave us like this. You're my husband and our child's father. You cannot just walk out on us," Mary cries, tears running down her cheeks.

She is still dressed in her church clothes. The three had arrived from service moments ago. The green dress is beautiful and even with red eyes and wet cheeks, Starr thinks her mommy looks pretty.

"I cannot do this anymore, Mary," Starr's father repeats, pushing at Mary's hands which are reaching for him, whether to hit him or hold on Starr cannot tell. Maybe both, she reasons to herself. "I love you," he continues, looking like he wants to cry too in his Sunday best. "You know I do but I am too young to have all this responsibility. I am only twenty-five years old yet most days I feel like an old man. I should be seeing the world, sowing my wild oats. Not working a dead end job or stuck in this town. I do not want to look back on my life in ten years and see that I have accomplished nothing."

"You call being my husband and our daughter's father nothing?" Mary's hands push at his chest this time, her anger rising.

"You know what I mean, Mary." Travis takes a step back but Starr does not think it is because Mary is strong enough to push him. He is much bigger than Mary with muscles that create bumps on his arms even under the long sleeves of his light blue shirt.

"I do not, Travis. I really don't. I thought we were happy. I know we married young and had Starr young but I would never give you two up for anything." She sighs then says in a more quiet tone, "I know we are struggling. Things could be better financially and stuff but as long as we stay together we can make it work. Please do not do this to us, Travis. Do not break up our family. You two are all I have and I can't lose either of you.

Please, don't break my heart, baby. Don't break Starr's heart. She needs her father."

Her tone is so pleading Starr cannot help but turn toward the couple completely. They are standing in the kitchen which is only one room over to where she is seating in the living room. The walls are yellow and bright, so different from the mood of everyone contained within them.

Travis hesitates and both Starr and Mary hold their breaths, waiting for his next words.

He goes in close to Mary and takes her hands. Starr feels a burst of warmth in her chest, wondering if things would be okay now. Her dad leans down to kiss her cheek.

Even from her spot, Starr hears when he whispers in Mary's ear, "I am sorry. So fucking sorry."

Mary jerks in his hold like he has struck her but does not say anything else.

She turns her head away but Starr knows more tears are falling from her eyes.

That warmth Starr felt in her chest fades away leaving an ache behind.

Travis lets go of Mary's hands then comes over to Starr. He picks her up, gives her a hug and kisses her forehead.

"You know daddy loves you, right, princess?" he says against her skin. "That will never change."

Starr nods and whispers, "I know, Daddy."

"Bye for now, baby girl," he says, not looking her in the eye as he begins to pull away.

Her small hands clutch at his clothes for a bare second before she lets go.

"Bye-bye, Daddy," she returns his farewell. Even though her eyes burn hotter, she still does not cry. She cannot even if she wants to. The tears seem to be stuck inside her.

Travis puts her back in her spot then crosses back into the kitchen without another word to Mary who is still where he left her.

He grabs his coat and puts it on. He does not look back when he turns the lock.

"I'll be back for my things later."

That is the last thing he says before leaving the house, and the two females behind.

The door shuts softly and the house rings with the sound of finality.

It is suddenly very quiet. Starr can hear the tick of the clock and the gentle hum of the refrigerator.

She watches her mother and the woman is frozen on the spot for a few seconds before her head starts to swings back and forth in a silent denial of what just happened.

She suddenly screams the word. "No!"

Startled, Starr sees her mother crumble before her eyes. The woman folds into herself, hands clutching her middle as she falls to her knees.

Without a clear thought, Starr finds her little legs pushing her across the room and she falls to her knees next to her mother. Mary is crying hysterically and Starr rests against her, instinctively comforting.

Mary reacts and pulls the little girl close, burying her face against Starr's curly hair. She clutches tighter than is comfortable for Starr but Starr does not complain. Instead, she strokes her mother's light brown skin and long hair.

"It is okay, Mommy," she consoles, wondering if it ever will be again.

CHAPTER ONE

A thirteen-year-old Starr wakes up slightly disoriented from a dream-filled sleep.

The images instantly disappear from her mind as she looks around. The familiar sight of the digital clock at her bedside flashes 6:31 AM and it sinks in that she is in her bedroom, safe and sound in her bed.

She yawns and stretches, sinking deeper into the mattress of her twin bed. The springs creak a little with the movement then settle as she lies still, hugging her pillow and inhaling the familiar scent of the fabric softener. Looking out the window, she sees the dawn breaking as she takes a moment to just lie in the semi-darkness. Soon though, longtime habit has her pushing the covers aside.

She is ready to start the day and her feet hit the floor with the beat of a young lady determined to be productive.

After taking care of business in the bathroom, she goes into the kitchen, fully expecting to prepare breakfast but to her surprise her mother, Mary is already there, stirring a pot on the stove. Not only that, Mary is humming and shaking her hips slightly. Her pleated skirt, part of her work uniform, sways with the upbeat motions.

Shocked, Starr stays still for a moment, unsure what to make of this scene. She and her mother had developed a routine over the last few years and Mary being up at this hour is not part of it.

Mary works as a waitress and often comes home late at night due to covering a late shift. Starr had taken it upon herself to make breakfast a while back to allow Mary to sleep in for at least a few more minutes. Sometimes, she even left for school while Mary was still in bed.

While this is unusual behavior for Mary, Starr is very happy to see this change in her mother.

Her mom and dad have been divorced for about four years. Mary changed when the man left.

Even at the age of only seven, Starr recognized that the light and life that had made Mary such a vibrant woman had been drained from the woman with Travis's departure.

For a few weeks after Travis left, Mary had been in constant state of distress, often in tears. But eventually, she pulled herself together and made a life for Starr and herself as best as she could.

Still, she remains a shell of the perpetually happy woman she used to be.

Starr had not seen the man for over six months. His calls are more frequent than his visits though. As a matter of fact, Star had spoken to him just last night

The conversation had been brief and slightly awkward. So very far from the easy and carefree manner they interacted when she was younger. Before he left.

Starr determinately shook off the negative thoughts. She tries as much as possible not to think about the estranged relationship between her and her father or that of the one between her mother and father. It is better that way.

"Hey, Mom. What's going on?" she asks as she steps further into the kitchen, still in her PJs.

Mary turns around with a bright smile. Her straight hair is pulled up into a ponytail that makes her look like a teenager herself. It bounces with the bubbly movement.

"Oh hey, honey bear," she greets her daughter. "I didn't hear you. How did you sleep?"

Okaayy is Starr's thought at this super cheerful Mary.

Even faced with this strange behavior, she rolls with the punches and answers, "I slept great. How about you, Mama? I did not hear you come in last night."

Mary's shift ended at 11:30 PM last night. Starr had already gone to bed by then.

"Oh, I slept wonderfully!" Mary exclaims and bacon sizzles as she adds it to the pan after sharing the eggs that she had scrambled between two plates.

She places bread in the toaster. Mary continues to make breakfast and Starr pitches where she can, unused to being inactive in the kitchen.

The two settle into an easy way rhythm until breakfast is prepared and dished out into two plates.

They both dig in and their conversation dwindles into nothing. The silence is suddenly punctuated by Mary saying, "So…"

It is a sound heavy with meaning and Starr looks up with a forkful of her eggs on the way to her mouth. She eyes her mother. Between Mary's strange behavior that morning and the way she looks at her now, pensive yet delighted, Starr becomes worried. She puts down the fork, eggs uneaten and forgotten.

"Is something the matter, Mama?" she asks.

Mary opens her mouth to speak but nothing comes out as if she cannot find the right words.

A few seconds later she tries again and blurts out, "There is someone

I would like for you to meet. Actually, he is coming over today. He is a really nice man and I hope that you two can get along."

More silence is broken by the tick of the clock on the wall. Their home has not changed much since Travis left and that same clock had ticked during the final hours Travis spent here.

Starr is waiting for her mother to add more to that statement but none is forthcoming. In fact, Starr gets the sense that Mary is waiting for her reaction.

She doesn't know how to react until it dawns on her that her mother is speaking about this *he* in a romantic way.

Oh. Oh.

Still, she had to confirm.

"You mean you're dating someone?" she squeaks.

Mary's cheeks brighten then become pale as she fiddles with her napkin and pushes her uneaten breakfast about her plate.

"Well yeah, uh I mean no… Kinda," she says in a rush.

She takes a breath and stops fidgeting. Then she puts her hand over Starr, which is on the table.

Looking into Starr's eyes, she tries again and says, "What I mean is yes, I am dating someone. He is a very nice man and we have been going out for about a month now. I like him. A lot. He makes me feel…"

She paused as if to gather her thoughts then continues, "That does not matter. What matters is that if you don't like him, that will be the end of that and I will stop seeing him. You're the most important person in my world Starr and your happiness comes first."

Mary squeezes Starr's had to punctuate her meaning but all Starr sees is her mother sliding back into the dark state she has been in for the last few years.

So she answers, "I am sure he will be just as nice as you say, Mom."

Even though the thought of having a man around — one who is not Dad at that - is a foreign concept, she silently adds.

Mary beams with that affirmation from her daughter and in a burst of energy gets up from the table to clear away her unfinished plate.

"Great," says Mary as she grabs her bag and jacket. "I've got to run a few errands before I get to work so I have to run but I am so happy that you are okay with this, baby girl."

Her parting words end with her kissing Starr on the forehead.

She heads for the front of the house with a pep in her step and soon Starr hears the door open and close.

Starr watches her mother until she is out of sight, wondering at her strange behavior and this strange man she is going to bring about.

Soon though, she forces it out of her mind. She needs to finish her breakfast and get to school.

Starr prides herself on being early to school every day. Far more responsible than most girls her age, Starr is a straight-A student, tutors a few of her peers and helps out in the community without prompting. It is no surprise that she is well liked by many in the small town of Idlewild, Michigan.

About twenty minutes later she shuts the front door behind her and tugs her backpack higher on her back. She meets up with her cousin and friends and walks to the bus stop.

Starr is seated at the kitchen table.

She has been home for almost two hours now, coming straight here after school. Her face is buried in homework when her mother opens the door later that day. She has an exam tomorrow that she is determined to get 100% on.

She is signaled to the arrival of Mary by the sound of the key in the lock followed by footsteps but does not look up, memorizing a diagram in the textbook.

She sees her mother enter the kitchen in the corner of her eye and her concentration is broken.

She finally looks up. She automatically responds to the huge smile on Mary's face but the show of teeth freezes when she sees that Mary is not alone.

There is a man with her and he towers above her 5'8" frame. Starr does not have a great view of him from this angle but she sees that he has broad shoulders and straight teeth with a brief smile. He is dressed casually in a polo shirt tucked into khaki pants.

"Come in, come in, Pierre," Mary ushers him and he steps further into the kitchen. "Starr come meet the nice man I told you about."

Starr gets a better view of him and the first thing that pops out at her is his light brown eyes. They are piercing and so bright against his chocolate brown skin. A light stubble frames his pink lips and his close-cropped hair is gently waved.

Starr stands up from her position at the table. It would seem that she is obeying her mother's summons but the move is defensive, although she cannot place why she feels threatened.

The space suddenly feels too small and too tight and for a moment she cannot breathe.

She sucks in a breath when Mary says, "Pierre I would like you to meet my precious daughter, Starr. Starr, this is my special friend, Pierre. He will be hanging out with us every now and then. As long as you're okay with that."

The two adults are close and Pierre offers his hand. Good manners dictate that Starr shake it and she does so automatically.

His huge hand swallows her smaller one. She tries to control the shock that passes through her but feels like she fails. He is so very warm that his palm feels hot against her. His skin tone is darker than her caramel one and his palm is rough against hers. Starr swallows the lump in her throat and says politely, "Nice to meet you."

There is another flash of straight teeth and Pierre replies, "Same here, young lady. I must say your mother's description of you does not do you justice. You're even prettier than she said."

Starr feels her cheeks warm at the compliment and the twinkle in his eyes as he says it.

He squeezes Starr's hand as he says this. The pressure is brief and not uncomfortable but definitely notable to Starr.

"Mary, you have a truly beautiful daughter," Pierre cements. Then, as he drops Starr's hand and glances at Mary, adds, "She comes by it honestly then, with a woman as stunning as you to call her mother."

Mary's cheeks turn a brighter shade and she giggles like the girls in Starr's classes did when they are discussing boys and stolen kisses when no one is watching.

"Oh, before I forget, I brought you these, Starr. I had no idea which one to get you but I have a daughter around your age and she likes these so I was hoping you do too."

Starr had not noticed that he kept one hand behind his back until he suddenly conjures a bouquet of flowers. They are white lilies. She takes them and says, "They are nice. Thank you."

"I'll cook us dinner," Mary offers. "Let me help you," Pierre chimes in.

Starr puts the flowers in a vase, then in the center of the table. She clears away her books and tells the adults she is going into her room to continue with her studies.

They hardly play her any mind. The last thing Starr sees as she disappears into her bedroom is Pierre touching Mary around her waist and whispering in her ear.

His gaze briefly flashes back to Starr before it focuses entirely on Mary.

Mary's light laughter echoes in the house that has long been absent of the carefree sound.

Starr gets on her bed and tries to refocus on her books. Mary's laughter continues to drift to her along with the soft murmur of the male voice.

Starr feels antsy. She is sure she should be happy that Mary has found someone who makes her happy but something prevents her from feeling so. She is unable to give her complete attention to her studies no matter how hard she tries.

Finally, she gives up, flops back onto her back and stares at the ceiling.

It seems like a long time yet not when she is called back into the kitchen.

"Starr come out here, please. Dinner is ready," Mary calls. Dinner is a tasty concoction of meat and potatoes with a side of salad. Starr is sure of this. Mary is, after all, a great cook. Still, it tastes like cardboard in her mouth, her nerves not allowing her to enjoy the meal. She nonetheless spoons the fare into her mouth dutifully.

Starr is mostly silent as the adults fill the space with easy conversation. She speaks when spoken to but otherwise keeps her eyes on her plate and her mouth closed.

A sixth sense tells her she is being watched. Her eyes snap up and she finds Pierre looking at her.

Starr has been gaining much attention lately and it came in the form of the young boys around the neighborhood. Starr is blossoming into a woman and it shows in the way her body has been filling out. Her chest and hips are certainly more generous than last year and the clothes she had bought only a few months ago are too tight now, some downright indecent.

Pierre's stare feels like those boys' own. The ones who catcall every woman that passes by. Hot and predatory. Like a wolf on the hunt.

Starr gets the same embarrassing and uncomfortable feeling she did when those boys threw words that made her blush her way. "So Pierre," Mary begins and Pierre looks her way.

The conversation starts up against like a beat had not been lost. His stare is earnest and focused on Mary and for a moment, Starr imagines she imagined the hooded look.

Mary seems to light up as soon as his eyes turn her way, looking as happy as Starr has seen her since Travis left.

All Starr wants is for her mother to be happy again. And so she makes up her mind.

If she has to deal with this new man to make her mother happy then she would. It did not matter how uncomfortable she feels when he looks at her.

Later, close to 9 PM, when Mary and Starr are alone, Mary asks Starr, "What do you think of Pierre?"

They are seating in the living room. The dishes have been done and cleared away. Starr does not study again tonight but still feels confident that she will ace her exam. She always does.

The two ladies had been watching a bit of television before they retire to their respective bedrooms for the night. Mary turns down the volume then faces Starr.

Starr faces her mother as well, tucking her legs under her on the couch.

She watches the television's light highlight Mary's high cheekbones and pouty lips.

Her eyes are searching Starr's face.

Remembering the look on Mary's face when Pierre was around and seeing that anxious look now as she waits for Starr's response…

Well, there is no way that Starr will break her mother's heart by saying anything other than, "He seems very nice. I like him. You should bring him around more often."

Mary squeals with joy and hugs Starr close.

CHAPTER TWO

Four Years Later

It is a warm spring day. Summer is near and the scent if it is in the air.

Starr is on her way to school. She walks in single file on the sidewalk with her friends, Alyssa and Kandy, and Yvette, who is her cousin.

The foursome is discussing a juicy piece of gossip that is currently floating around their high school when the offensive comment booms through the air.

"Yo, ma. Give me your number!"

The audacious teenage boy not only hollers the insulting words, but he makes a grab at the seventeen year old girl dressed in her tightest jeans.

With her light color latte skin, long, wavy hair and bold attitude, this teenager is considered quite the catch in the neighborhood and she knows it. She is a self-proclaimed "bad bitch" and only the most confident guys hollered at her with success.

She looked at the youthful, thug wanna be with his baggy pants drooping below his behind, graphic tee embossed with graffiti art and the du-rag on his head and conveyed her thought.

She is so out of his league it is laughable.

He is beneath her and not worth her time clearly. How dare he try to touch her without invitation!

Yvette Jones neatly sidesteps the hold and spins around to land the boy close to her age with a glare that is shooting daggers.

"Excuse you," she says with a roll of her neck that women of color are famous for. Her hand goes her hip in a further show of her displeasure.

Making a cocky sound, the guy repeats, "You heard me, ma. Let me have that math. You know you wanna give it to me."

Yvette looks back at her group and says in a tone dripping with disbelief, "Does this lame really think I would ever, even if he was the last man on earth, give him the time of day? Please tell me he is not that dumb."

The crew behind him start to snicker, sensing the upcoming blowout and their friend's subjacent rejection.

There are a total of seven males including the forward instigator. Starr recognizes a few of them from her school and knows the rest of them as high school dropouts just hanging about on the block. They all range from the age of fifteen to early twenties. Starr feels the heat of one of the other boys look and his eyes catch hers. He licks his lips in a suggestive manner and she flushes at the attention before looking away.

Starr's figure has only gotten more voluptuous over the years. Her thick thighs, an ample butt, and a slim waist are 100% god given.

Of course, a figure like hers earns the lusty attention of many men, young and old, and she has been proposition plenty. She should be used to the attention by now but she still gets a little rush every time she realized that a man is admiring her as a desirable woman.

Whereas a few years ago she would have wanted to go hide from the attention, she liked it now. So of course, she pushed her chest up a little and cocks her hips to highlight her curvy derriere.

The boy immediately zooms in on the press of her breasts against her soft, pink sweat.

She is feeling a little turned on from the attention and she feels her chest tighten. Her bra is a thin lace material and she wonders if the points are visible through the sweater's cloth. She knows they became big like pencil erasers when she was feeling like this. She thinks maybe they are when he tries to subtly elbow another male next to him and gesture at her.

She almost giggles, getting a heady rush from teasing the boys. Boys are so predictable. Tease them a little and they become putty in her hands, sniffing around her heels like lost puppies. All these guys can do is look though. She does not need or want his touch. She already has someone more than willing to touch her in places that give her far more than heady rush, and he is not pimple-face, inexperienced these boys are.

Yvette turns back to the boy with a saucy movement and Starr almost feels sorry for him because she knows her cousin is about to cut him down to size.

Starr suddenly realizes she knows him. He attends one of her accounting classes. Roland is his name. He is usually a far more subdued character. She guesses being around his friends gave him the courage to make a move on Yvette.

"First of all," Yvette starts. "You need to back the fuck out of my space real quick. Don't let this pretty face fool you. I *will* kick your ass if you ever dare to touch me without my permission again."

She let that sink in before continuing, "Second, that quick line was lame as fuck. Don't use it again. On any girl. And third, ewww. You and I will never, ever — and I do mean never - happen so get that thought out of your head."

With her speech complete, Yvette turns her back on the slack-jawed youth who is turning red with embarrassment. The other boys behind him guffaw and tease him as Yvette rejoins her group of friends who high five her as they laugh at the rejected male.

They continue 0n their way to school like nothing happened because that scene is after all pretty much a normal, everyday occurrence, with any one of them getting harassed by a hopeful, horny young man.

Starr throws a look over her shoulder to find her admirer staring at her ass as she walks away. He smiles at her, realizing that he has been caught and feeling no shame.

Starr turns back around with a roll of her eyes but barely holds in a giggle.

"You sure told him off," she tells Yvette.

Yvette rolls her eyes and replies, "As if I would ever take on the likes of him. I need me a real man, honey. One who knows how to work it."

She gyrates her hips and makes a suggestive face and the girls peel into giggles again.

Kandy chips in her five cents on the topic. "Oh I know what you mean, honey. These little boys need to gain a few years and a whole lot more experience to handle me."

She does not hesitate to throw in a piece of gossip as she pops the gum she has been chewing.

"Y'all hear that Michelle roped herself a "real man"? He is almost thirty I hear."

Michelle attends the same high school they go too and had already turned eighteen a few weeks ago.

"I more than heard. I actually saw them together last night. I was working my shift at the gas station when this Bentley pulled up and she was in the passenger seat looking all kinds of comfortable," says Alyssa.

She works part-time at one of the local gas stations, saving up for college. She has already been accepted by a cushy college in New York and cannot wait to hightail it there.

"I hear he is married too. Not only that. Their affair has been going on for months," she adds.

The other girls make sounds of disbelief at the juicy news, not noticing that Starr keeps quiet at the announcement and looks away.

"Oh please, y'all are acting so scandalized but I know y'all bitches are hella jealous of her right now. Am I right or am I right?" Kandy says with a raised eyebrow.

Yvette has no shame when she admits, "You're so right, honey. I would give my left tit to rope me a man like that."

More giggling ensues as the girls reach the schoolyard and are joined by more girls.

Starr goes about greeting the newcomers automatically but her mind is far.

What will her friends think if they know that she is messing with an older man, she wonders.

She smiles secretly, already envisioning the next time she sees her secret beau.

Starr simply cannot wait!

It is hers and his little secret for now. Harboring the secret makes it all the more exciting to be with him.

Not even the fact that he is married or cheating on his wife with another woman dampens her excitement.

CHAPTER THREE

Starr is dressed in a yellow gown.

She is beaming at her reflection in the mirror. She twists this way then that and her smile only grows bigger as every angle becomes more and more flattering.

"This is *the one*," she breathes a breath of wonder.

Prom is only two weeks away and after going through what feels like hundreds of dresses, she has finally found *the one*. She and her mother are in her bedroom, with two discarded dresses on the bed. She had already tried on those and one look told her they were not the one.

There is still one more dress to try but Starr is already certain that she found the best one of all.

"It is definitely *the one*," Mary agrees before coming up to loosely embrace her stunning daughter from behind. "You look so beautiful. No, you are more than that. You are just gorgeous. It seems like just yesterday you were my little baby, so tiny in my arms. I remember it like it was yesterday but now just look at you. You're growing into such a bright young lady, I thank God every day that you are mine. You make me so proud and I know that you will do great things."

Mary is emotional and a tear leaks down her cheek even though her smile is dazzling.

"Really, Mama?" Starr asks.

"Of course, baby. You are my bright little Starr and I know one day you will shine the world with your light. I know it is silly but seeing you in that dress makes it really hit home that you will be going off to college soon. I am going to miss you so much." College.

She had already been accepted to a college in California on a full scholarship.

It was something Starr had looked forward to going to for a long time. She had dreams of becoming a doctor, of leaving this small town and seeing the world, of accomplishing so many things... Now, thinking about it put knots in her stomach. Her whole life is in this small town and she does know if she can leave it all behind. Leave *him* behind...

She keeps her conflict to herself though and smiles at Mary, cooing, "Awww, Mama. That is so sweet. I am going to miss you, too."

Starr is touched by her mother's words nonetheless and turns so they can share a hug with more words, tears, and smiles.

Starr removes the dress and steps back into the jeans shorts and tank top she had on before. Mary is placing the gown back into its holder when knuckles rap against the front door

Knock. Knock.

Who is that? Starr wonders, with an inkling of whom it might be. "I'll get it," she tells Mary, already on her way to open the door. "Thanks, honey. I'll just put these dress away."

Pulling the front door open confirms Starr's suspicions. It is her mother's longtime boyfriend, Pierre.

He has not changed much since she met him five years ago except that he now wears his hair cut even shorter and is sporting a neatly trimmed beard. He looks even more distinguished now.

One thing that such has not changed is the intensity he looks at her with. She feels it heat her clear through her skin.

He steps inside and instantly dominates the room. His presence is so large that she expects nothing less.

"Hey, Pierre," she says breathily as she pushes the door shut. "Hey, baby girl," he says back.

He looks the teenage girl up and down, giving her all kinds of kinky looks that go straight to her head… and other parts of her body.

See, things have changed in the last few years Mary has been dating Pierre. Instead of being uncomfortable with his heated looks, Starr now looks forward to them and the hot tingly sensations they send through her body.

They make her feel like a woman. Like doing the things a woman does…

Her mind gets lost imagining just what these things are. Mary yells from the back of the house, "Who is it, Starr?" Starr's forbidden and totally depraved reverie is broken by her mother's voice.

"Oh Mom, it's for you. It's Pierre."

"Send him back here, Starr," Mary returns. "Okay," she yells in her mother's direction.

She turns back to the handsome man and says softly, "You know where to find her."

"I know," he says. "But what if I came to see you instead?" He steps closer to Starr with every word until his hard chest brushes her' own, where is rising and falling with her increasing excitement.

"I would like that very much," she whispers, thoroughly caught under this wicked man's spell.

"Are you not going to give me a welcome kiss then, little lady?" This is breathed against her parted lips.

"You know we can't. My mother is only a few room over. We will get caught."

He puts his hand between her legs. Only the fabric of her shorts and panties prevents contact with her lady bits, which are decidedly a little bit damper since he stepped inside. He bends down and licks the exposed part of her cleavage. She barely bites back a moan despite her earlier words.

"But that is half the thrill of it, Starr baby," Pierre says.

Starr was only sixteen years old the first Pierre touched her in a place her mother and school counselors told her is a "bad touch" zone. It was on her thigh, close to the edge of her pantie line.

He, Starr and Mary had been having dinner. They did so intermittently when Pierre could break away from his wife. The fact that Pierre was and still is married to another woman is a secret the three kept.

The conversation had been steady when he suddenly touched Starr under her skirt under the table where Mary could not see. Starr had not protested, though initially startled.

Despite the uncomfortable feelings Pierre had incited in her when she was younger, she has grown used to his heavy hooded looks and the small touches on her shoulders and hands by then. In fact, she had found herself looking forward to and craving his attention soon.

They made her feel special. They still do and the feeling increases every time they do something totally forbidden and taboo.

When dinner was over, with Mary putting away dirty dishes, he had told her that the touch was their little secret.

Even though she had felt bad for keeping secrets from her mother, she had agreed.

Pierre had only grown bolder since then. And now she touches him back.

But this is cutting it too close. Mary can walk in on this naughty play any second.

She slaps Pierre's hand away from her crotch and steps out of his hold, saying, "Stop that, asshole. Do you know how much trouble we can get into if mom catches us? She will be mad and hurt."

But even she hears there no real conviction in her words.

"You like it, girl" Pierre smirks, knowing what game she is playing. "Besides, that has never stopped you before. You know you want me bad."

Although Starr is playing hard to get now, she bites her lip thinking about going all the way with Pierre.

They only had not yet because of Pierre. He wants to wait until she was of legal age.

"I can get into a lot of trouble if someone finds out we had sex before you turn eighteen," he told her once when she whined about him teasing her then not going through with it.

He had appeased her by saying, "We can play around still though. No harm in that."

And play around they do.

She cannot wait until she turns eighteen in two weeks so that she can fully become a woman in every sense of the word under his care and attention.

She flushes hot just thinking about it.

Still, she opens her mouth to tell him off further but just them Mary barges in.

She looks at Starr with a frown. "What happened? I told you to send him back here, baby. Oh hi, Pierre. I missed you."

She goes up on her toes to give Pierre a habitual and quick hug and mouth to mouth kiss.

"I missed you too, baby," he says smoothly as Mary settles back on her feet.

There was no clue that he had been fondling Starr seconds before.

Starr is not as good at playing the role and cannot find her tongue to give a proper excuse.

Starr is frazzled and knows that Mary notices but her mother does not say anything for which Starr is thankful.

That is mostly due to Pierre diverting Mary's attention by saying, "I was just telling Starr that it is very admirable what a beautiful and smart young lady she is turning into. Just like her mother." Mary laughs at the compliment and Starr joins her, although the sound is forced.

Mary pats Pierre's chest affectionately and her touch lingers in familiarity. Starr zeros in on the action. Her smile freezes on her face and an insidious emotion is stirred inside her.

Pierre is dressed in his work clothes – a dress shirt and slacks over shined shoes. His tie is loosened and his jacket has been discarded somewhere along the way. He always looks good – no great.

Starr is sure he could be dressed like a homeless person and he would still rival the models on the covers of magazines with those honey colored eyes and pink lips that know how to work her into a frenzy.

He works out regularly and has an amazing physique to show for it. And man does she love when he shows it to her!

He is older than her by more than two decades but she is convinced that the fact is part of his appeal. His age comes with sophistication and experience that make boys her age pale in comparison.

She wants to slide up against him every time she sees him. But lately, she wants to shout to the rooftops that he is hers.

She wants to claim him and that means no other woman had the right to touch him like Mary is doing.

Starr's laughter falls away as the jealousy makes her vision narrow at the edges.

It is a feeling she has been experiencing with increased intensity. And one she is having increased difficulty reigning in.

She has always known that she has to share Pierre with his wife and with her mother but lately, the more her feelings for him evolve, the less she feels inclined to do that.

"You are such a charmer. It is one of the things I love best about you," Mary says to Pierre, looking up adoringly as she guides him to the back room.

Pierre throws her a heated look and a wink over his shoulder and she gets giddy all over again. Not even the distance murmur of Mary's voice as the pair disappear or the knowledge that she is betraying the woman who gave birth to her dampens the feeling. Starr has discovered that lust is stronger than her love for her mother or the sense of guilt intertwined in the mirage of feelings contained within her young body.

CHAPTER FOUR

"I've been keeping a secret from you guys but I cannot hold it in anymore."

Starr did not mean to blurt that out but it came out without permission from her brain and now her two friends and cousin are looking at her expectantly.

Starr has never had a serious boyfriend and now she has an adult man chasing after her... Well, she is surprised she kept in in at long

"Well, spill it, girl," Kandy becomes impatient with waiting when a full thirty seconds pass and Starr says nothing more.

The four girls are hanging out at Starr's house. They are all posed in various positions on the bed with Starr sitting Indian style, with her back propped with pillows against the headboard.

It is later that same day. Pierre had not stayed long for his visit. He had stopped by on his lunch hour and did not have much time.

Mary is now preparing herself to work a four to eleven shift tonight. She should be leaving any minute now. Mary still works at the same restaurant but has been promoted to a supervisor now.

She had promised Pierre that their affair would be their little secret but now that she has let the cat out of the bag with her friends, she has to spill all the beans and her friends will gobble them up, she knows with certainty.

She leaves out the part about Pierre being married though. This has been a secret she and Mary have kept for so long it is now ingrained in her to do so.

Kandy blurts out, "Girl, you are lying! He has been grabbing your ass and feeling up your tits and everything?"

"Yup," Starr confirms. She is smug with the admission and the other girls are in an uproar at the juicy details.

They get too loud and Starr is afraid that the noise will alert her mother and she shushes them.

They all look toward the bedroom door but it remains as it was with only a slit keeping it from closing. Mary is nowhere in sight. Yvette injects, "And you have not told you mom about this?" "Hell no, you idiot," Starr denies. "I want to see how far he will go. Besides, it is so exciting! Having all that man hot for little ole me."

Yvette is not sipping on all this tea like the other girls are and concern marks her face.

"You really need to be careful, Starr. Your mom with be devastated if she finds out about this. Aren't you worried about hurting her? She has done so much for you, working herself to the bone to ensure you are well cared for. Especially since your father hightailed it out of town. She does not deserve this." Starr does not appreciate Yvette's tone and opens her mouth to tell her off but suddenly Mary pushes the door open.

"Okay girls. I'm off the work now. Be good, y'all hear."

"We will. Bye" everyone chorus with trying to hide the varying degrees of guilt on their faces.

All that is except Starr. She has long since learned to deal with that emotion and hides it well, notwithstanding her slip that afternoon.

Mary does not notice a thing amiss and leaves the house soon after.

"You know what, I don't believe you. You're too much of a goody two shoes to do something like that. You have not even fucked a boy yet and now you're going around messing with your mother's boyfriend? I don't believe that."

Those words come from Alyssa. They bring up similar disbelieving looks on Kandy and Yvette's faces and Starr cannot have that. Not at all.

So she says, "I'll prove it to you. I'll call him up right now."

She gets the cordless telephone and rings Pierre's work line. The ringing sound fills up the space as she puts in on speaker. All the girls gathered around to listen in on the call.

When the line is picked up, she says, "May I speak to Pierre, please?"

There is a pause then Pierre says, "Speaking, Miss Starr. What's up, baby girl?"

"You recognize my voice?" She smiles.

"Of course, baby. How can I not when that voice makes me hard every time I hear it? My lust for you is so great, it is almost painful. Imagine how good it will be when I get inside you."

Alyssa's eyes widen at Pierre nasty words and Kandy covers a gasp. Satisfaction fills Starr.

Told you, bitches! she thinks.

Pierre laughs. "Are you calling to find out what a horny bastard I am?"

"You've just been on my mind and I wanted to hear your voice," she says.

"I've been on your mind, baby, huh? I like to hear that. I bet all your thoughts have been naughty. Are you ready for me?" he purrs and the heat in his voice goes straight between Starr's legs. "You know me too well," Starr returns seductively.

"That I do, baby girl. Is your mother around?"

"No, she left for work a little while ago. Are you going to visit me?"

She does not tell him that she has company.

"I think I might do that. Just to check up on you. To make sure you're all safe and sound. Would you like me to do that, baby girl?"

It is a risk they often took. He would come visit her under the guise of making sure all is right with her while her mother is at work.

"Oh yes. I'll be waiting with something sexy on. Something that will make the big man in your pants happy to see me."

His groan comes across the line. "Damn, girl. You know how to get me right on edge. I'll be there in a few minutes."

He hangs up and the dial tone sounds.

Starr ends the call with an excited sigh.

"Ohhh, girl. You are sure a slut!" Kandy cries and Starr suddenly remembers that she is not alone.

She had called Pierre to prove a point but hearing his voice… He had become the center of her universe and nothing else mattered. Just like always.

She scrambles off the bed and heads for the door.

"Sorry girls, excuse me while I shimmy into something sexy. I'm expecting company in a little bit," she boasts proudly.

The look on Alyssa and Kandy's face are exactly what she is looking for – envy – and it strokes her ego.

Yvette's face holds a different look. Like she is seeing Starr for the first time and she does not like what she sees. Starr ignores that look and turns away.

Yvette's voice is the last thing she hears as she leaves her bedroom.

"Starr girl, you are playing with fire. Watch out or you might get burned."

She goes into her mother's bedroom and straight to the closet. She pulls out a short skirt, one she has never seen her mother wear but still stores away in her wardrobe.

There is a special collection of these clothes in the very back of Mary's closet. They are relics of her younger years with Travis and Starr now uses them to seduce Mary's current boyfriend who is married to another woman.

She quickly shucks her pajama pants and matching top. To make herself feel even sexier she removes her panties as well and they land on the pile of her discarded clothing.

She pulls on the skirt, which is made all the shorter by her generous curves, and a sequined top that makes her breasts look spectacular.

In the mirror, she fixes her hair. She piles the curls on her head to expose her shoulders. She pulls a few tendrils free to frame her face.

Using Mary's makeup, she makes a smokey eye and paints her lips bright red. She busses her lips and practices sensual expressions.

Her naughty play is interrupted by a soft knock on the front door. She quickly puts on a borrowed pair of heels and leaves her mother's bedroom with cat-like swagger to her hips.

The other girls do not hear the noise, making a ruckus in her bedroom.

Not wanting to share her time with Pierre with anyone else, Starr quietly makes her way over to the front of the house.

Leaning against the door, she asks softly, "Who is it?" She swallows a giggle. As if she doesn't know!

"Don't play games with me, little girl. Let me in," Pierre answers with a mock growl.

She does giggle then.

She loves the way his expression that darkens his face when she opens the door and he sees her.

He steps into her space and closes the door behind him. He does not give her time to say anything.

He grabs her and pulls her to him. His lips cover hers and she opens up for his invasion with a needy sound.

The kiss is frantic. It scares Starr a little. Pierre has never lost control like this with her before. He has also directed their naughty play in a way that told her he is holding back.

He is not holding back now and she doesn't know how to handle this aggressive passion.

She puts her hands on his shoulders, intending to push him back but then he pulls his head back to look down at her with those intense eyes.

"You're so fucking gorgeous. I find myself needing you more and more every day," he rasps in a rough tone that scrapes her nerves in just the right way.

She finds her fingers digging into his shirt instead to pull him closer. Their tongues tangle again and she has no thoughts of stopping this time.

He pushes her up against the nearest wall and his hands push her top down to cup her full breast. She is so very ready for his touch.

He pushes a leg between hers and drags her hips forward and her molten core is brought up his thigh. Her sensitive skin is abraded by the rough contact but she loves the feeling.

Her wetness smears against the fabric of his pants and she is delighted that he will smell of her even when he is gone.

They begin to dry hump each other, both breathing heavily. In fact, they are damn near panting at this point.

Pierre leans down to take her dust colored nipple into his mouth. Her head falls back against the wall as her mouth opens with a silent scream at the rush of all-consuming sensations.

His hand goes under her skirt to find her bare.

"Fuck," he breathes against her lips. "I can't hold back this time. You are too tempting."

This is it, she thinks, high on bliss. *He is finally going to take me.*

Both their hands go to his belt, pulling and undoing.

The buckle clunks and then the *zzzz* of a zipper being undone sounds.

Starr dips her hand inside his pants and feels his hot hardness through his underwear.

He cups her ass and lifts her easily. She automatically wraps her legs around his waist. His hand moves between them and then his hot length touches her plump neither lips.

He is poised at her entrance then- "Starr, where are you?" Yvette calls. And just like that, the spell is broken.

"Fuck, why didn't you tell me someone else is here?" Pierre angrily whispers.

Starr is too turned on right now to speak.

Pierre quickly lowers her back to her feet. He tucks his privates back into his pants and zips up.

He looks at Starr then and his eyes look her up and down where she leans against the wall. Her legs are wet noodles and she needs the support.

Her hair has fallen free from the updo and her breast is still exposed, pushed up and down by her heaving chest. Her skirt is high enough on her hips to show off the neatly trimmed strip of hair guarding her unpenetrated sex.

She is quite the sight and knows she has an effect on the wanton man even now. His eyes hold the same burning desire she feels despite his anger.

"Damn, the things you do to me, little girl. I gotta go," he says, pulling her skirt and top back down into place. "Hold that thought for another time."

He gives her one last hard kiss on the lip and one second later he is gone, leaving the scent of his woodsy cologne behind.

No sooner he closes the front door does the three other girls find her. She has yet to move from her position.

"He was here?" Yvette asks.

"I would say so," Kandy answers for Starr. "She looks like she has been fucked within an inch of her life. Damn, that man must be a sex magician to work all the magic in only a few minutes."

Starr smiles, ignoring the sour look on Yvette's face.

"He sure is," she says and Kandy and Alyssa giggle with her.

CHAPTER FIVE

The next morning brings a huge surprise for both Mary and Starr.

It is a Saturday and both Starr and Mary are at home when someone knocks on the front door.

After Pierre's visit last night, Starr and her girlfriends spent many hours talking until the other girls went to sleep around 2 AM. Starr had been unable to sleep at all and had lain awake, thinking about how close she and Pierre had come to actually going all the way. And how disappointed she is that they had not been able to.

She covers a yawn, the effects of not getting a wink of sleep getting to her since it is already 10 AM. She is lounging on the couch, after having excused her tiredness with coming down with a bug to her mother.

Mary is taking the time to get some cleaning done and is wiping down the kitchen cupboard when the sound of the visitor's arrival echoes through the home.

"I'll get it, honey," Mary says to Starr.

Starr makes a sound in the back of her throat, barely able to muster the energy for even that. She has no plans of moving from her spot in a hurry.

"What are you doing here?" Starr hears her mother say.

The odd note in her mother's voice had her rising and going up behind her mother, tiredness forgotten.

"Oh," is her mutter of surprise. "Hi, Dad."

"Hey, ladies. How are you both doing?" Travis asks with a huge smile on his face.

Travis has changed a lot since he left ten years ago. He had filled out and become even bulkier with tattoos.

Travis is a very good looking man with an air about him that told people to tread carefully. It might have something to do with the fact that he had been to prison a few times and bounces between bouncer jobs He even runs with a motorcycle club.

There is a small amount of grey at his temple.

His smile softens his features and makes him more approachable.

"I'm okay," Starr replies and cannot help repeating her mother's question. "What are doing here?"

Mary does not answer his question, her eyes searching his face. For clues at his unexpected visit, Starr suspects.

"I should have called before I stopped by but I wanted to surprise my girls," Travis answers Starr.

My girls? Starr thinks and she notices Mary's eyebrow rise in the same puzzlement she is feeling.

"Oh," Mary answers. "Well, it certainly is a surprise. Come on in then."

Everyone moves into the living room and pleasantries are exchanged.

Travis hands Mary a bouquet of flowers and Starr a small wrapped present.

"Oh, these are beautiful and my favorite too. You remembered."

Mary's brings the daisies up to her nose for whiff as she gushes. "Of course. I remember everything there is to know about you. You're not a woman that is easy to forget."

Mary's eyes jumps to Travis's own and widen.

The two do not say anything verbally but Starr feels like a silent conversation is occurring with their visual connection.

The silence stretches until Starr clears her throat in discomfort. The adults hastily break the connection and Mary says, "I'll just put these in water," indicating the flowers.

She walks the short distance to the kitchen and reaches into a cupboard for a vase.

Travis turns to Starr then with his smile in place.

"Are you going to open your present?" Travis's asks Starr.

She tears the teddy bear decorated paper and to reveal a necklace with a star pendant. It really is beautiful and Starr thanks him. However, she does not feel much as she accept the gift. Travis always brings a present when he comes to visit but they are poor consolation for him not being around much.

"It will be time for lunch soon. I was just about to prepare something. Would you like to joins us, Travis?" Mary says a few moments later.

"I'd love that," he eagerly answers. "Let me help you." "Oh, okay. Peel these potatoes for me please."

Travis gets to the assigned a task and the two get cozy preparing the meal.

They include Starr in their running conversation and Starr wishes she had not lied about being sick so she leave. She loves her father but she did not feel comfortable with his presence anymore. He is gone way too often for her to feel that way.

As it is, she is stuck lying on the couch to rest as her mother has directed.

Starr takes the time to observe the interaction between Travis and Mary.

Travis is acting strange.

Normally when he visits, Starr gets the feeling that he cannot wait to leave.

Today is different. Starr senses no such urgency in him. In fact, he is looking very comfortable in the space like he intends to stick around for bit.

He is laughing and touching Mary quite a lot also.

The touches are not obscene – on Mary's hand, arm and shoulders – but they are often enough for Starr – and Mary no doubt - to take notice. Mary does not protest though and Starr notices a blush on her cheeks often.

These two are sexually attracted to each other even after all these years and it is plain as day to see.

Ewww, Starr thinks, turning her head away. *I might have to gouge my eyes out.*

Yup, she definitely wishes she can be anywhere but here.

The three spent a few hours together until Mary mentions that she has to prepare to get to head out for a bit soon.

Travis hesitates to leave but ultimately goes to the door with Starr and Mary in tow.

He gives Starr a hug and a kiss on her cheek.

Then he turns to Mary and repeats the action. He holds onto Mary longer though and keeps possession of her hand when he lets go.

"I'll be seeing you guys again soon," he says. "I have to head up to Atlanta for a few days to tie up some loose ends but I'll be in town for… a while after and I hope it is not an imposition if I stop by once in awhile."

After Travis's words, there is a moment filled with uncertainty and there is a look of hope on his Travis that Starr does not understand.

"Of course," Mary says. "You're always welcome." Travis is smiling now and so is Mary.

Starr feels like a third wheel.

"You have no idea how much I love to hear that," he says, his eyes on Mary.

His touch lingers on Mary's hand and the two adults share another moment Starr's does not understand.

Soon Travis leaves and Starr puts the moment out of her mind. Whatever it was is of no consequence.

Starr does not expect to see him again soon despite what he said. He always disappears for months after a visit, with only his calls to punctuate his absence.

CHAPTER SIX

It is later in the afternoon.

Alyssa, Kandy and Yvette are staying over for the night again. Mary has just finished a shower and is in her bedroom getting dressed to head out to do some grocery shopping.

Alyssa and Kandy are eager for an update on what is happening with Pierre and ask Starr to call him up again.

Yvette is off to the side, hardly participating in the conversation. Starr ignores her, shucking her behavior off as jealousy.

"He is so much of a man, girls. Listen. Kandy don't laugh, he might hear you," Starr boasts as the phone rings. She had called his workplace and was informed that he had taken the rest of day off. So she dialed the number to his house.

A strong male voice comes across the line a few seconds later. "Ford residence. Pierre speaking."

"Hi, Pierre. It's me, Starr," she says, trying to sound sultry. Starr is imagining that he will be thrilled to hear from her, especially after last night. Instead though, a stern tone comes across the line.

"You should not call this number. I told you this before. You are taking a lot of chances, Starr. Just like last night," he says.

Starr quickly diverts his attention. One, because she hates it when he is mad at her and, two because she didn't want him to reveal the fact that he is married to the audience that he unknowingly has.

"Don't be mad at me. I just needed to hear your voice. You know I always miss you like crazy when you're gone." He sighs and the deep sound echoes.

"Damn it, you know I can't stay mad at you," he says. "Not when you get my blood up so quick. You blew my mind yesterday. I always knew you had that fire in you but last night… phew!"

He trails off and make a suggestive sound.

She giggles and Pierre starts to say something else when there is suddenly a noise on the line.

"Starr, I need to use the phone," comes Mary's voice. Frantically Starr calls out to her mother, "O-oh, okay, Mom. Hang it up, hang it up."

Luckily, Mary does what she asks but still Starr's heart races with the near miss.

⸺ ∞∞∞ ⸺

In the kitchen, Mary leans up against the kitchen counter and stares at the telephone mounted on the wall.

Her forehead is knitted in puzzlement.

I know that male voice on the line, she says to herself, trying to place the voice she heard when she picked up Starr's call.

A few seconds later she is no closer to solving the puzzle and give it up.

She picks up the phone to place a call to Pierre. She dials his home number, knowing he got off work early today.

The line is busy so she tries again.

The call connects this time but the person who picks up is not who she expects.

Pierre's wife, Karen picks up the phone. "Hello, who is this?" she answers.

Mary does not miss a beat even as her heart skips a beat before going into hyperdrive.

"Hello, may I speak to Ronnie please," she asks, deliberately asking for a wrong name.

Karen's tone is sharp when she tells Mary, "You have the wrong number."

The two women hang up. Mary sighs.

She know she is not setting a good example of righteousness for Starr by dating a married man but it is easy being with Pierre. Even though he has promised that he will leave his wife for good eventually Mary knows he will not. And she is okay with that because she is not looking to get married or into a serious relationship again even though she has found that she has grown attached to him over the years. She tried that once and it did not work out.

She did not want to put her heart on the line again. Speaking of her heart…

Travis's face flashes through her head and she quickly shakes the image away.

Her silly little heart is still pining over that heartbreaker and she has no intention of going down that rocky rock with Travis even if she had a feeling that something is different with him when he visited earlier.

A few minutes later she heads out the door with a farewell call to the girls, her mind blissfully empty of her troubles.

Well, apart from trying to figure out who is that man that Starr was talking to on the telephone.

CHAPTER SEVEN

It is prom day.

The day so far has been magical for Starr.

She was awoken by her mother with a special breakfast in bed treat and has been treated like a princess all day with a spa treatment with her girlfriends, manicure and pedicure, lunch at a high-end restaurant sponsored by Pierre... the works!

She is on cloud nine especially since Pierre has made many appearance and whispered lovingly in her ear while sneaking in touches Mary does not see.

It is late in the afternoon now and Starr is getting ready with Mary's motherly help and affection. Pierre is around the house, popping his head into Starr's room every now and then to see how things are progressing and of course, sending admiring praise Starr's way.

It all sounds very fatherly for Mary's benefit but he winks and blows kisses to Starr behind Mary's back.

It is all Starr can do not to giggle and give them away.

Early evening rolls around and Starr is all dolled up. The same yellow dress hugs her figure lovingly and contrasts wonderfully against her light brown skin tone.

Her hair has been professionally styled into an updo that exposes the delicate line of her neck and pronounces collarbones. Her skin simmers all over from special lotion while strategically placed jewelry glitters from her ears, neck and wrists. Her facial features are more pronounced with makeup highlighting her best features.

She is gorgeous.

Mary gushes over her and Pierre gives her that heavy hooded look. Another giggle almost escapes Starr when she catches a glimpse of the bulge in his pants.

For me? She mouths at him since Mary is near.

Always, he mouths back and discretely adjusts himself. Just then the doorbell rings.

"That must be Marlon. Pierre, can you get that please," Mary says as she makes last-minute adjustment with Starr's dress.

"Of course, darling," he replies and Starr scowls at the endearment but he sends another wink her way before going to do Mary's bidding. Just that easy Starr is in high spirits again. Marlon is Starr's date for the prom and one of the most popular kids in school.

She could not possibly say no when he asked her to the event, especially when she knows how much so many of the girls at school lust after him. To get asked by him is quite the status booster and Starr laps it up even though she has no real interest in him otherwise.

Why would she went she has a real man making her feel giddy with his secret pursuit?

The two males come into the room and the contrast is sharp. Marlon is a star swimmer and even got a full scholarship to a renowned college based on his abilities. He is in great physical shape and has a handsome face. Standing next to Pierre though, he looks immature and pales in the looks department.

"Goodness gracious, Starr you look amazing! I am going to be the luckiest guy at prom with you on my arm," Marlon compliments, coming closer to Starr.

"Thank you, Marlon. You are too kind," Starr replies, blushing at the admiration.

"Not at all. Just being honest," he charms and it is clear to see why all the girls want him at the high school. He pulls out a small flowered arrangement and asks Starr, "May I?"

She gives him the go ahead and he puts the corsage in her wrist and takes her hand.

Starr glances up just in time to catches Pierre frown at Marlon's touch.

Oh jealous, is he? She thinks, loving the thought. Now he knows how I feel whenever I have to watch him and Mary love it up. She holds the boy's hands tighter and he beams at her attention. "Oh, you two make such a cute couple," Mary adds, watching them with happy tears shimmering in her eyes. "Isn't that right, Pierre?"

He makes a rough should in the back of his throat. "Cute, yeah." "You two had better get going. You don't want to be late," Mary says.

Mary leads the way.

Pierre trails behind the young pair as they head to the front to meet the car that is there waiting to take them to the venue. Starr feels Pierre touching her ass but acts normal, not giving him up. She even presses into his touch for a brief moment before stepping out the door.

After an emotional goodbye, Starr is driven off while Mary and Pierre fade in the distance.

— ⚭ —

When Starr is gone, Mary and Pierre reenter the house. Mary shuts the door and looks at Pierre in his face

"My girl is a young lady now," Mary boasts, ever so proud. "She certainly is, Mary. She certainly is," he agrees.

Mary ventures further into the house with happy expression and does not notice the angry scowl Pierre throws in the direction the car went.

The lustful expression on the boy's face as he looked at Starr made Pierre want to destroy something, particularly Marlon's face.

CHAPTER EIGHT

Starr is just entering the house when the telephone rings. She came straight home from school and as soon as the door closes the door when the sound echoes.

She already knows who it is.

Quickly dropping her backpack on the floor she races for the device.

"Hello?" she greets breathlessly.

"Hi, my baby," comes Pierre's seductive voice. "Are you ready for your big day?"

Starr can hardly contain her sigh as she leans against the wall. It has been two days after her prom and Pierre has been especially attentive. She knows that it is because he thinks that she might have some interest in Marlon. She does not.

They hardly saw each other on the night of prom mostly because she stuck with her girlfriends and made up excuses for why she did not want to dance with him.

She knew that Marlon realized that she is not interested in him by the end of the night.

He took it like a good sport though, with a kiss on the cheek at end of the night when he dropped her at her front door.

She is not about to tell Pierre how very plutonic everything was though.

She likes this possessive side of him.

Mary is at work until late tonight as both she and Pierre well know and she does not have to hide her words or actions as she speaks with her man.

"Yes," Starr answers Pierre, knowing he is referring to her eighteenth birthday which is only about a week away. "I will be a woman finally."

"I can't wait," he replied, his tone dropping and sending the most delicious tingles down her spine since she knows exactly what he cannot wait for.

Before she can answer, a beep on the line tells her another call is coming in.

She is tempted to brush it off but knows that it is likely to be Mary. She does not want her mother getting worried and coming home early so she tells Pierre to hang on while she takes the call. "Hi honey," Mary says. "Just making sure you got home alright. How was your day?"

"Oh fine, Mama. I'm a little tired so I think I will turn in early tonight," Starr replies, adding a yawn for good effect.

"Oh well, don't let me keep you then, baby girl. Get some rest and don't forget to lock up tight before you head to bed," Mary adds.

"I will," Starr pacifies and ends the call.

Back to her conversation with Pierre, she asks him, "When can we see each other again, Pierre?"

"I'll try and make that happen soon, baby. You know I miss you."

"Not like I miss you," she says. "Or else you would be here me right now. We have the place all to ourselves until my mom comes home after eleven tonight."

She is pouting and does not care if he hears it across the line. In fact, she wants him to. She wants more of his time and affection. A few heartbeats pass then he gives her what she wants.

"Okay, my baby. I'll be there in a few minutes. An hour, tops," he says.

Starr squeals with delight and makes kissy noises.

True to his words, a knock on the door about half an hour later announces Pierre's arrival.

Starr rushes to answer.

Pierre does a double take when she opens up for him and says, "Wow."

Starr is barely covered in a short black dress she confiscated from her mother's closet.

He steps inside and the door closes to cocoon them in an air of lust and desire.

He encloses Starr in his strong arms and she leans into him as he presses kisses along her neckline and shoulders. His hands cup her behind and squeeze before pressing her into him.

"One day it will just be us two. We will not have to sneak around like this," he murmurs against her skin.

As if Starr is not already drunk on his presence, those words further intoxicate her. That is want she want too. This man, all to herself.

The next few hours are a dream come true for Starr. Pierre has all his focus centered on her and she is addicted to him. They talk, laugh and of course, touch.

Her dress has long since ridden up her silky thighs and the thin straps are pushed off her shoulder.

The two are on the couch, Pierre lying partly over her. Her thighs hug his hips and they are kissing passionately.

She is slightly frustrated though. She wants him to lose control like he did the last time and finish what they started. But he keeps on pushing her away every time they get close.

She is determined not to let that happen again and tries to undo his belt.

While she is barely clothed, he has not removed a stitch of clothing except his shoes.

He stiffens as soon as she makes that move and gets off her. Starr gets off the couch too, not even thinking to pull the dress back into place. It remains bunched over her hips like a thin scrap of fabric and her tiny panties and lace bra mold her curves.

"Pierre," she starts but he cuts her off.

"Be quiet," he says roughly. "You're just too fucking tempting right now. I have to get out of here before I do something I should not. I'll call you later."

With that, he slides his shoes back on and heads for the door.

She is shocked by the abrupt turnaround from the affectionate and attentive man from minutes ago. She does not move from her spot for a while. Not even when she hears the front door open or sees Pierre take off in his SUV without even bothering to close it.

The clock ticks minutes by and she remains in that position trying to figure out what just happened between Pierre and her just now. The feelings swirling inside her have immobilized her. She is furious.

She is sad. She is hurt.

She is in love… and right now she hates it.

The sound of another vehicle brings her muddled mind to the surface slightly and as if from a distance she sees her father coming out of a car that just pulled up into the driveway.

Travis rushes in and she still she does not come out of her daze. It is not until he yells, "Starr! Starr! What the hell is the matter with you?" that she comes back to the present fully.

Mortified, she runs into her bedroom with a cry to cover up her body.

She dressed in a tee shirt with a Disney character embellished on the front and a long pair of pants. Running her hand through her hair, she seats on her bed and tries to pull herself together.

She stalls for as long as possible, hoping Travis leaves but when she returns to the living room, he is there. The front door is firmly shut.

Travis immediately comes over to a subdued Starr and starts firing questions.

"What's going on with you?"

"Is someone messing with you?" "Are you dating?"

"Did a guy hurt you?" "Who is it?"

"Why were you standing there like that - dazed and confused? Anyone could have come in here and taken advantage of you." "Are you using drugs?"

Already unhappy at Pierre for his abandonment, Starr is tempted to unload her bad mood on her father.

How dare he just badge in here like he has the right and ask her all these questions? He is hardly ever here and if he thinks he can just come in here and act the devote parent then he is sorely mistaken.

Why is he even back so soon? She expected a few months to pass by before she saw him again.

She really should tell him off.

Instead though, she just says, "No, no, no. It is nothing like that. I was just getting undressed when I heard the door. The lock must not have caught when I closed it early. I just spaced out for a few seconds."

She ducks away from his probing gaze and goes to the refrigerated for a bottle of water.

There is a pause before Travis says, "Okay, fair enough."

He clearly knows something is up. It shows on his face. But Starr is too drained to worry about what he is thinking.

"Did you need something?" she asks, hoping she can figure out that is so she can send him on his way.

All she wants right now is to be alone.

"Actually, I need to speak to your mother. I'll just wait around until she gets home," he answers.

Stomping down her anger and panic, Starr says calmly, "She will be back quite late since she is working a late shift. You should probably come back tomorrow."

"No, I'll wait."

With that statement of finality, Travis settles in on the couch, looking far too comfortable for Starr's state of mind.

She barely keeps from rolling her eyes and stomping her foot. "Fine, whatever," she says and goes to her bedroom without a backward glance, locking the door.

That is, not before she grabs the telephone. Pierre has some explaining to do.

———— ⚬⚬⚬ ————

Across town, Pierre wife, Karen is observing her husband's behavior as he sits out in his SUV in the driveway talking on his cell phone.

From inside the house, she is watching him through the blinds and her heart breaks with every second that passes of the more than thirty-minute call.

He only just arrived home since leaving that morning. She had called to let her know he would be working late but a call to his job dispelled that lie. But then she had already known otherwise. Being at work has been his excuse a lot for coming home late for the past few months but more often than not, simply picking up the phone would inform her otherwise.

For a long time, she tried to deny the obvious but she cannot anymore.

Her husband is cheating on her.

From the light of the cell phone, she can see that he is smiling and gesturing animatedly. He looks happy. An emotion he has not directed her way in quite some time.

She and Pierre have been married for almost two decades. At first, they were so in love. He showered her with attention and his affection.

Then, their daughter, Anya came and things changed. Although he is never mean or derogatory to their daughter, he became distant and Karen has yet to figure out a way to get emotionally reconnected with her husband.

And now, she suspects him of having an affair.

He glances up eventually and catches her spying on him. His eyes widen before he drops them but she saw the guilt in the split second.

That look confirms her suspicions and she feels a heavy pain bloom brighter in her chest.

She drops the blinds and heads toward her bedroom. She has seen all that she needs to.

⎯⎯ ✺ ⎯⎯

Pierre quickly ends the call as he sees his wife's shadow move across one of the downstairs windows.

"Um, I have to go Starr. I have to go inside," he says.

He does not give her chance to answer and presses the red icon before exiting the car.

A few minutes later, he comes through the front door of their two-story colonial style house in the suburbs.

The lights have been turned off except for the one on the foyer. He breathes a sigh of relief, thinking maybe he saw wrong. Karen and Anya should be asleep anyway.

He drops his car keys and wallet on the table near the door and undoes a few buttons of his shirt. The action sends a whiff of Starr's perfume up to his nose.

He gets lightheaded as all the blood in his body rushes to the center.

Damn it, this is not the time or place for these thoughts, he tells himself, trying to settle down.

After locking up, he moves to head up the stairs and nearly jumps out of his skin when he notices Karen seating at the bottom in her nightgown.

The look on her face is disturbing, vacant and harsh.

"Why are you taking calls outside in the car?" she asks quietly. "It was a business call," he answers, falling back on his usual excuse.

She gets up from her position and comes up to him. Looking him dead on the eye, she says, "I know you better than you know yourself. Good night, Pierre."

With a mean glare, she goes up the stairs. Shortly after, the slam of a door echoes.

Pierre stands there for a minute then hangs his head with a sigh. He then heads for a downstairs restroom to clean up. He will take the couch tonight. He has no intention of sleeping next to all that hostility.

In the shower, his mind is in turmoil thinking about his failing marriage. He wonders if partaking in these adulterous relationships will finally come back and bite him in the ass.

He is not worried about Mary causing him trouble. He knows that she accepts that he is married and will not interfere. He knows that she will never approach or confront his wife. He knows that she will never show up at his house.

Mary is not looking for anything deep with him. She just wants a companion since she is lonely.

But Starr...

Starr, on the other hand, is a wild card. She is impulsive, emotionally driven and capable of doing anything.

Even though that cannot board well for a future relationship, those qualities excite him and he feels himself harden just thinking about the young lady.

His mind becomes solely focused on Starr and their forbidden love affair.

She makes him feel young again. It is a thrill to secretly pursue her and he finds himself unable to give up the feelings that come along with that even though he knows he should end it.

He cannot though.

She is forbidden fruit and he needs to have a taste... or perhaps gobble her up entirely.

He starts stroking his hardness, thinking about her nubile body. He cannot wait until she turns eighteen years old.

Shortly after his release splatters on the tiled wall of the shower but he feels far from satisfied and he knows he will not be until Starr is woman enough to take him.

CHAPTER NINE

A worn out Mary comes home.

Her feet hurt, she has a raging headache and all she wants to do is go to her nice, soft and warm bed.

Pierre has helped her and Starr financially over the years, furnishing the home and even buying Mary the vehicle she now drives.

He has told her more than once that she never has to work again. He wants to take care of the two of them.

But she insists on working and making her own way even if the work is hard and backbreaking. She can at least set *that* good example for Starr.

She is expecting to find an empty living room since she figures Starr will be asleep.

It is eleven forty-six PM on a school night after all.

Instead, she jumps in fright spotting a male figure leaning back on the couch.

"Oh my gosh! Travis, what are you doing here? You startled me." He rises with a flex of muscle that never fails to make her heart… and other place flutter.

She ignores the feeling. She has a lot of experience doing that. It is a little harder to block out the heady scent of cologne and man, but she still manages.

"I didn't mean to do that, babe. I'm so sorry," his deep timbre comes.

He comes up to her and pulls her into a quick hug.

She lets out a quiet gasp as the heat of his body penetrates hers. He has been acting really strange since he showed up a few days ago. He is looking at her different and getting really handsy.

This change has her both excited and nervous.

"What's going on?" she asks him, as she takes off her coat and places her bag to the side.

He fills her in on what happened with Starr when he got here. "She really had me worried, Mary. The look on her face terrified me. Is there anything going on that I don't know about? Is it a boy? God forbid, drugs?"

Truth is, Mary is worried about Starr. The teenager has changed as of late, running hot and cold at the drop of a dime. She used to be so sweet and caring all the time but now Mary has noticed hostile looks and snarky words are coming out of Starr's mouth more and more often.

Still, Starr is a teenage girl with the moods and hormones that come along at that age. Mary figures she will just give her space and everything will be just fine.

She explains as much to Travis, adding, "Starr is a good girl, Travis, with a great head on her shoulders. She will be okay. This is just a phase. All girls go through something like this at one time or another."

"I'll have to take your word for it. You know her better than I do," Travis gives in after a beat.

They just look at each other for a few seconds and the moment become awkward until she offers him a drink.

Minutes later though, the two have settled down and are having a deep conversation about everything and nothing. She shows him pictures of Starr on prom day and the two gush over how pretty Starr looks. He tells her about his plans to move back into town and set up shop. She is surprised at this move, not sure what to make of it and what it means for the three of them.

Mary lets out a yawn, very tired now.

"It is late. I should probably head out," Travis says. The clock reads 2:17 AM.

He does not sound like he wants to go anywhere. "Where are you headed to?" she asks.

He named a town over an hour's drive away and before she thinks about it she offers to let him stay.

"Are you trying to seduce me, Mary? 'Cuz you know I don't get down like that. You have to at least buy me dinner first before trying to get me into bed," Travis tells her with a sly smile.

"On the couch, I mean," she stammers, feeling her cheeks heat like a virgin schoolgirl. How embarrassing!

"I'm just teasing you, babe," he adds, making her cheeks get even hotter.

She slaps his arm gently and tries to hide her nervousness. "Oh, I know. Let's get you all tucked in."

She goes to get him pillows and a blankets, thankful for a moment to compose herself.

———— ✸✸✸ ————

Travis watches Mary walk away, the sway of her behind absolutely captivating his attention.

She has already gotten the sleeping supplies and the two have made a nice area for Travis to sleep on the couch.

His body is always primed when in her presence and it is especially so tonight with the closeness they shared.

He is pulled out of his lusty daze when he realizes that she has suddenly stopped moving. He figures he has been caught looking by the rosy color of her cheeks.

She does not call him out though. Instead, she softly says, "Good night, Travis."

"Good night, Mary."

She closes the door softly.

Travis knows that he was an idiot for ever having left his family and deeply regrets it.

Unfortunately, he did not have that insight when he was younger. He cannot lie though, it was fun for a while — being able to do whatever and whoever he wanted but the thrill wore out quickly. Pretty soon, he found himself making bad decision after bad decision. He has been to prison for a few petty crimes, has bounced around from state to state and job to job.

And it through it all, he has never found that peace he only found lying in Mary's arms.

He is at that age where he realizes that he need to get his shit together and step one in that is getting stable financially and job-wise.

He already has that in the works. He loves working on motorcycles, something he discovered after he left town years back. He found a job in a popular local shop a few minutes ride from here. Eventually, he will open up his own shop.

Step two is reconciling with both Mary and Starr.

He wants nothing more than his family back and he will do everything in his power to get his wife and daughter back. Mary is his first and only love and he needs to find a way back into her heart.

They were high school sweethearts and married and had Starr young.

They had been so in love and no one including him thought they would ever split up.

He is not sure how he became blinded to that fact and become focused in the huge responsibility of raising a family so young. Dumb and not seeing the value of what he had, he had ran out on Mary and Starr but now he needs to show the two that he is a changed man who will do anything to make them happy.

He need to convince Mary to allow him close enough to give him that second chance.

He has one more trip out of town to tie up some loose ends then he is back for good.

He smiles in the dark, already envisioning having his girls back.

CHAPTER TEN

The next morning, Starr gets up and comes into the kitchen groggy-eyed.

Even after her phone call with Pierre, where he claimed to run off because she is just too tempting for him to control himself, did she settle down enough to sleep.

She spent most of the night tossing and turning, growing aggravated at one turn then sweet-eyed with her need for this man at the next.

The result is that she has woken up from no more than three hours of sleep in a very rotten mood.

She spots Mary in the kitchen as soon as she enters. Her mother has started making breakfast and the smell of eggs and bacon filled the air, making Starr's stomach growl.

She walks straight to the refrigerator and grabs a carton of juice. "Good morning, Starr," Mary says cheerfully, grating on Starr's nerves.

With barely a glance at Mary, she replies, "Hey."

She notices a movement out of the corner of her eye and spots her father on the couch.

She almost spits out the juice she just drank.

"Good morning, Starr," he says, eying her disapprovingly, no doubting having heard her dry reply to her mother's greeting. "Oh uh, hey Dad, what are you still doing here?" she cries. "Your mother and I were sitting here last night talking and it got kind of late and she offered for me to spend the night instead of driving. I accepted and slept on the couch. No worries," he explains.

The two adult share a look before Mary turns away with a blush. Starr's eyes narrow, brain calculating.

Her bad mood evaporates as she comes up with a few conclusions that will make her life a whole lot simpler. Mary and Travis getting back together will eliminate one obstacle in the way of she and Pierre being together exclusively.

"Oh," Starr goes. "Well, it's good to see that you are here, Dad. You're staying for breakfast?"

"Yes."

Breakfast is a merry affair with the three seating around the table, eating, laughing and talking. Anyone looking in from the outside will think they are the perfect little family.

Their perfect little union is broken up by a sharp knock on the front door.

When Mary opens the door, it reveals an angry looking Pierre. "Oh, hey Pierre! What is going on?" Mary exclaims, clearly shocked because he hardly ever stops by so early in the morning. At the reveal of the unexpected visitor's identity, Starr forks falls from her suddenly limp fingers and makes a loud sound against her plate. She makes eye contact with her father then and notices his curious looks.

She quickly drops her gaze before he sees too much. Luckily, he does not voice any of the questions she saw in his eyes.

"Oh, just curious. I drove by and saw a strange car in the driveway and thought I should check up on you and Starr. What's going on? What are you guys doing this morning?" he replies cooly as he steps past Mary and comes inside like he owns the place.

Mary closes the door with an apprehensive look on her face. Pierre knows about Travis and what he looks like but Travis is clueless as to who Pierre is and what he means to Mary and Starr.

Travis stands up and holds his hand out even though his gaze has anger beneath the cool he is projecting.

"Oh hi, man. How you doing?" he asks.

Pierre looks at Travis, then at the offered hand but does not accept it.

"How am I doing? What are you doing here?" he snaps, stepping into Travis's space aggressively.

"You got a problem, man?" comes Travis's equally hostile reply. "Because we can take this outside anytime you're ready."

Mary is having none of that in her house though and steps between the two men.

She is facing Pierre when she says, "Whoa, whoa, whoa! You are very much out of line, Pierre. This is Starr's father. He wants to spend time with her and I do not appreciate you badging in here with that kind of attitude. What is wrong with you?"

"I know exactly who this fool is. What I want to know is whether or not he just got here because he looks awfully cozy for the deadbeat dad he is."

He looks over at the sofa with it disheveled pillows and blankets. Someone obviously slept there.

Mary's hands go to her hips and her body is vibrating with her anger now.

"I don't come to your home and question you about what you are doing. Why are you here questioning me about what I am doing?" she yells at him.

Throughout the confrontation, Starr does not say anything. In fact, she is still seated at the table and continues to eat her breakfast as if this big blowup is not happening right in front of her. She can hardly keep from smiling and giggling at the entertainment.

Her bad mood is completely and utterly gone.

All she can think is, *he is going to be mine. I can feel it.*

"Girl, who do you think you are speaking to like that?" Pierre is getting really angry now and he steps closer to Mary.

Travis quickly moves Mary away and behind him, shielding her with his body. His stance changes and he is wired to move at the drop a bat.

"Yo man, back up," he growls.

Travis is the bigger man and is obviously hardened in a way that Pierre is not.

Pierre looks him up and down and suddenly says, "Fuck this. I don't have to deal with this bullshit."

He turns around and walks out the door.

Mary pushes from behind Travis and makes a sound that conveys disgust and disappointment. Sucking her teeth, she runs after Pierre, dodging Travis's hand.

Travis stays close to her, standing in the doorway and watching what is going on between Mary and Pierre.

"Wait, wait, wait," Starr hears her say to Pierre. "Why are you mad? What is going on? You've never acted like this before."

Starr can just imagine Mary clinging to Pierre on the front lawn as he goes to his vehicle even though she cannot see anything from her vantage point.

Then Pierre's voice comes, "I know you slept with him last night, Mary. I just fucking know it."

"We did not sleep together last night. I promise we did not," Mary says. "You can ask him."

There are no more words then a vehicle starts up and there is the screech of tires as Pierre leaves.

Mary comes back inside shortly after and goes into her bedroom with the slam of the door but not before telling Travis, "I think it's better if you leave now."

He does not protest, only giving her worried, angry look. Breakfast is obviously ruined and Travis packs up to go.

On the way out, he hugs Starr and says, "Bye, baby girl. I'll be back soon."

Cheerfully, Starr says, "Bye, Dad. Hope you and mom work it out."

He gives her a strange look before closing the door behind him. Soon the sound of his car backing out of the driveway is heard.

It is not long before Mary comes out of her bedroom dressed in her uniform.

"Where's your father," she asks Starr and she replies, "Oh, he left."

"O-oh okay. I'm off to work. Your father told me what happened last night. Are you okay being by yourself?"

"Of course, Mom. Don't worry so much. It was just a freak accident. The door lock had not caught on properly. But nothing happened and I will be more careful. Promise."

"Okay, baby." With a hug and a kiss, Mary leaves.

As soon as the sound of Mary' car dies, Starr hurriedly gets the phone and dials Pierre's number.

He answers immediately and says, "Baby, I've been waiting for your call for so long. Your stupid mother keeps calling me and I know that she has been fucking your dad."

Starr cannot let this opportunity pass without throwing a little shade at the competition and replies, "Oh yeah, they're fucking. They were fucking all loud on the couch last night."

Pierre goes, "Oh yeah? I knew it!"

After a pause, he continues, "Well baby, I'm all yours. I'm not dealing with your mom anymore."

Starr smirks, feeling as if she has won.

Pierre is all hers now…

Then Pierre says, "You know what? I'm on my way back there. You just be ready. We're going to go someplace special today. I'm going to leave work and we're going to go somewhere. Just you and me finally."

Starr is giddy with excitement and happiness, jumping up and down. They have never been out on a date before.

She ends the call with Pierre with the promise, "I'll be ready and waiting."

She has to tell someone about this and dials Kandy's number afterward.

"Kandy, I'm getting ready to go on a date with my man," she tells the other teenage girl gleefully.

Kandy says, "Who?"

Starr rolls her eyes. This girl can be a bit dumb at times. "Pierre," she says.

Instead of the encouragement she is expecting from Kandy, the other girl says, "Come on Starr. Aren't you taking this a little too far? You're not seriously going to date your mom's boyfriend, are you?"

"Well, it's over between them because she's fucking my dad and Pierre popped up this morning catching them in the act," she informs Kandy, the lie falling off her tongue easily.

After a bit, Kandy replies, "Oh, I did not know your mom was cheating on Pierre."

Starr's tongue has no bones this morning and she blurts her mother's business out, "Well, technically, my mom is not cheating on Pierre because he has a wife."

"Oh wow," Kandy says, stretching the last word. There is silence on the line then she adds, "Well Starr, I have to go now. I have to do something for my mom."

"Okay," Starr says, not liking how unexcited Kandy is with her news. The two hang up.

Starr showers and snags another sexy dress from her mother's closet. By the time she is done with high heels on, dressed fitted and makeup and hair snatched, she looks like she is out for a night on the town.

When Pierre calls, he says, "I'm outside baby, come on. Let's go." "Be right there, babe," she answers.

She locks the door behind her and walks the short distance to Pierre's SUV. She loves the dazed way he takes in her outfit.

———— ∞ ————

Pierre watches Starr approach him and feels like he is in a movie. As if in slow motion, she moves, her hips popping and breasts swaying with her cat-like movements.

His heart quickens and the shaft between his legs throbs to life. He feels like he is in high school again, picking up the hottest chick in school for a date.

So he does what a proper date would does.

He jumps out of the vehicle and runs around the side to open the door for Starr. He helps her into the passenger seat.

"Hi, babe," he says when he is seated next to her.

"Hi, Pierre," she answers, breathily, licking her juicy lips. He cannot resist going in for a kiss.

He barely finds the strength to pull away and not drag her into the house to have his way with her. She tests his control even more when she looks at him with those sex-filled eyes.

"I have a great day planned. You're going to love it," he tells her and she beams with happiness.

Minutes later, they drive away with his hand high on her thighs and his mind filled with all the ways he can make this young girl addicted to him just as he finds that he is addicted to her.

⸎

Neither of them notice the blinds at the neighbor's house shift or the eyes that widen and the eyebrows that lift as the neighbor connects the dots.

This neighbor picks up the phone.

Such a juicy piece of gossips needs to be shared right away.

CHAPTER ELEVEN

It is Saturday morning and Starr's eighteen birthday.

Starr does not like celebrating her birthday and has not ever since Travis left. Therefore, the day usually passes with her lounging around and exchanging a few gifts with Mary at dinner time.

At first, Mary had insisted on parties and elaborate gestures to make Starr pass the milestones but eventually, she realized that the celebrations made Starr more miserable than happy and dropped it.

This morning, Mary had prepared a lovely breakfast and handed Starr a gift card for her favorite clothing store, thinking she can spend the day shopping.

Now, she is rushing to get to work on time.

Mary is almost out the door and says, "I'm out of here Starr. See you when I get off work. Enjoy your big day."

"Thanks, Mom. See you later," Starr says absent-mindedly.

Her mind is on how she *really* wants to spend her big day. She just wants to spend her birthday with only one person. Her man. Pierre.

Too bad she is mad at him right now.

As if on cue, the phone rings with her thought.

She knows it is Pierre but she just stares at the device, not picking it up.

After their amazing day out together, where Pierre wined and dined her, he withdrew from her.

He hardly returned her calls and was short with her when he did. He did not come around the house much and their contact has been very limited.

To make it even worse, she knows he and Mary have been in contact and she has no idea what communication was exchanged. Are they getting back together?

Are they meeting up outside the house? Are they having sex?

With every question, her doubts and fears increase until she is filled with all these negative emotions.

Oh yeah, she is good and mad. Pierre has a lot of explaining to do and she will not be pacified with a simple phone call.

Turning her back on the ringing phone, she turns on the stereo, blasting the music loud.

She knows that when Pierre hangs up, he will try again and she did not want the annoying sound to invade her time alone. Humming softly at the sexy RnB song that is playing, she goes into the bathroom and turns on the shower.

She steps into the tub and not even five minutes into the activity, she begins bathing herself very slow and intimately while dreaming about Pierre. Even if she is angry at him, just the thought of him gets her hot like nothing else.

She is so absorbed in her fantasies and the elicit feelings they are enticing in her that she does hear Pierre enter the house or call her name even though he is making no effort to be quiet. Not even when he enters the bathroom does she hear him.

Her eyes are closed tightly where she leaning against the tiled walls and she does see him lick his lips at the sight of her wet nakedness. Nor does she see when he begins to shed his own clothing, his body already hard and aching with desire for her.

She is daydreaming of him touching her sexually — caressing her thighs, licking up and down her neck and back, stroking her womanly center…

He slides the see-through shower door back and she is startled. Her eyes immediately open and widen at the sight of him.

"What are you doing?" she yells, instinctively covering her breasts and lady's center with her hands. It is a very ineffective barrier if the lustful look on Pierre's face is anything to go by. Pierre steps into the shower and begins kissing her and his answer is, "Only what you want me to do."

Her lips, her necks, her shoulders, her breasts… he kisses it all as he moves her hands out of the way. They fall to her side and she unresisting. In fact, her head is thrown back from the pleasure of his actions and her body movies to make her skin more accessible to his talented mouth.

Still, she remembers that she is mad at him in the back of her mind and says, "Pierre stop."

The words are weak and unconvincing. He ignores them and she is glad for it when she hisses with the bliss of his nipping at her skin. His tongue quickly passes to soothe the sweet ache his teeth caused.

He squeezes passionately, turning her around so that her front is pressed up the wall. The cold of it contrasts sharply and deliciously with the hot feel of him behind her. He is driving her straight to ecstasy and there are no more words of stopping.

This is what she has been waiting for for so long and there is no way she is letting him leaving without showing her what it means to really be a woman.

He turns her back around and puts his tongue down her throat. They really get into then.

Grabbing the back of her thighs, he lifts her and braces her against the wall. He positions her feet on the edge of the tub, leaving her body fully exposed to him. She feels the hot slid of his maleness between her feminine folds.

He captures her lips once more and thrusts inside.

She screams into his mouth with the pain of her first time and he swallows the sound.

She is nervous now and tenses up. In all her imaginings of how this would go, pain never factored into it.

Taking his lips away from hers, Pierre strokes her back and hair. His hips are moving, going back and forth with sharp, deep movements.

"Calm down, baby. Just calm down," Pierre croons to her. "Relax yourself."

He moves faster, stabbing into her harder and harder. He is grunting and groaning, and his forehead is furrowed with the sensations that full his body.

Starr gets dizzy with the combination of pain and pleasure swamping her being and moans.

Pierre lifts her higher and she wraps her legs around his waist. This changes the angle of his presence inside her. His length hits something different inside her. Something that makes the pleasure overpower the pain and her moans get louder as she clutches him closer to her.

"Oh, Pierre," she cries out, watching him through her eyelashes. Her lids are heavy with this sexually experience.

"Yes, baby, that's it. Take it. Take it like a woman," he encourages her, pulling her against him every time he pushed into her.

He leans down to suck on her breasts, slowly biting her nipples.

When he bends over her, his slips from her body. She unwraps her legs from around him and he helps her put her feet back on the floor of the tub.

Instinct is guiding her and she grabs his shaft where it pointed from his body. It throbs with his desire for her and is slick with her moisture. There is the slick pink tinge of her lost innocence. She feels inexplicably proud seeing the evidence that she is now woman enough for this fabulous man.

She squeezes him and his maleness pulses.

He is so big and hard, she thinks in wonder.

She moves her hand up and down like he had shown her how to do in the past, jacking him off. She goes at a moderate pace at first then speeds it up.

He is the one to throw his head back in bliss this time. He makes sexy sounds in the back of his throat and leans into her motions. He is loving every second of her hot touch and she loves making him feel good.

All too soon he stops her though.

"Damn, baby, you are going to make me blow too soon," he jokes but his voice is strained.

He turns her around again and her front is pressed against the wall once more.

He guides himself back into her.

He is stroking her with a very sexy technique that has her moving with him. There is no more pain now, only euphoria. She is sure that she is now addicted to this ecstatic feeling he calls forth in her.

The feelings are building up in her body and she is anticipating a culmination that will leave her forever addicted to his man.

Then her mother's face flashes in her mind.

Guilt dampens her ardor and she says, "Pierre, we shouldn't d-do this."

She is having trouble getting her words out at this point. Still, she tries to do the good thing.

But then Pierre hits that spot inside her again – the one that make her dizzy with desire and love – and she forgets all about Mary.

Pierre gets to that point and shouts against her shoulder, "Ah, baby, ah. You make me feel so good. I never want this to stop." *Neither do I,* she thinks hazily. *Never.*

He reaches sexual satisfaction and there is a rush of warmth where they are joined. The rhythm of Pierre's hips become erratic. Still, it gives Starr what she needs to join him in this erotic paradise.

Starr has no idea how long passes but suddenly Pierre is taking away the presence inside her center.

It hurts a little when he does but she still shivers as a lingering tremor of pleasure passes through her.

He turns and dips under the still running shower.

Starr remains where he left her leaning against the wall for support. She is trembling all over and cannot move even if she wants too.

She watches him wash quickly, for the first time taking the time to appreciate his nude body since he stepped into the shower with her.

He does not glance at her the entire time.

When he is finished, he gets out of the shower and says, "Wait here."

He grabs a towel off the rack of extras and dries off quickly before putting his clothes back on.

And still, he does not look at her.

A feeling of foreboding makes Starr straighten from her position and she asks, "What it is Pierre? Is something the matter?"

Did I not satisfy him? she wonders in dismay.

He assures her, "No, there is nothing wrong," but those words and his tone does nothing to take away her doubts.

Just a few minutes ago, she felt like the most desirable woman in the world, now she feels self-conscious and less than a woman. Her nakedness all of a sudden feels wrong.

He walks out of the bathroom then.

Knees weaken, Starr slides down the wall and sits on the floor with the water beating down on her back. Between her legs throbs and begins to feel sore.

Time passes and Pierre does not return.

Only the sound of the music and the running water keep her company. Cold and apprehensive, she gets up on shaky legs eventually.

"Pierre, Pierre," she shouts out his name. "Where are you?"

She absentmindedly grabs a towel and wraps it around her body to ward off the cold. She continues to call Pierre's name as she leaves the bathroom and searches the home.

There is no answer.

There is no sign of Pierre anywhere.

She gets to the front of the house and the front door is cracked open.

She leans against the wood and her weight closes it. She does not need to check the driveway to know that he is gone. She feels it. Her mind is filled with questions, wondering what she did to make him leave like that.

How could he just leave me like that? she asks herself. She cannot come up with an answer to sooth the hurt.

The phone rings and she slowly turns her head to look at it.

Eyes still in its direction, she lets her body slide down the wall next to the door.

She feels numbness spreading through her mind and lets it take over.

Welcomes it, in fact. Anything is better than the tightness closing in in her chest and making it hard to breathe.

The phone is still ringing when she fades into a deep dreamless sleep.

CHAPTER TWELVE

Starr is awakened by the sound of her name being called and someone shaking her shoulders.

"Starr! Starr!" her mother's voice penetrates her subconscious. "Are you okay?"

Her eyes feel heavy and all she wants to do is bat Mary's hand away and continue sleeping. Still, she lift hers heavy lids to find Mary looking down at her with worry making her brows pulls together.

Behind Mary, she sees the front door open and the dark of night marking the sky. She can hear cicadas making the night's music and see a star twinkle.

The whole scene feels so distant, as if her mind is removed from her body.

For a moment, she is confused as to why she is on the floor in only a towel. Then, it all comes rushing back to her.

Pierre coming over.

Pierre making love to her. Pierre leaving.

She had fallen asleep by the front door and never woke up. The whole day had gone and she had done nothing but lie here.

Her eyes jump back to her mother's own and she searches them. Can Mary tell that she had been intimate with Pierre?

For a moment, she imagines Mary can tell just by looking at her. She almost wants Mary to just know. But logic penetrates the haze of guilt and possessiveness making her delirious.

Starr gets defensive since she feels guilty yet possessive of her new lover and snaps at Mary even as she tries to figure out if there is any evidence of what she and Pierre did.

"I'm fine. Quit touching me," she says sharply, pushing away Mary's searching hands and pushing herself upright against the wall.

Damn, her muscles are cramped from being in the same positions for so many hours.

Mary says, "Thank goodness. You had me so worried."

After those words, Mary stands with a look of anger mixing with her worry.

Hands on her hips, she starts in on Starr, "Get off the floor and get into bed. Why are you even sleeping by the front door in your towel no less? Why is the shower still running? You act as though you're on something, Starr."

Instead of paying attention to her mother's worried tirade, Starr is panicking in her head.

Oh my god. Oh my god.

The words keep on running through her mind.

Oh Lord, did I leave any evidence of what Pierre and I did? Did he leave his belt?

Is his cologne still lingering in the air?

One second ago she wanted her mother to know exactly she and Pierre did so she can finally claim him as hers. Now she is not so sure she wants to be confronted Mary alone if she does find out. How crazy is that?

She almost chuckles because she does feel crazy being pulled in so many directions emotionally.

"I don't know what has gotten into you lately but this has got to stop, Starr. The door was unlocked and you're lying here in nothing but a towel. What if someone had come in here and taken advantage of you? Did you even think of that? I can't trust you to be by yourself now and I know you're a responsible girl. So what gives? Where is this behavior coming from? Shit, I can't fucking deal with this!" Mary goes on.

Mary paces away and Starr rolls her eyes, mumbling, "I *am* on something. The man you think is yours."

She giggles softly at her own joke, her guilt vanishing like it had never been. She gets to her feet and does a visual sweep to make such there is indeed no evidence of the naughty things that went on the house earlier.

She hears Mary turned off the shower as she enters her bedroom and shuts the door.

Mary is upset.

After a hard day's work, she is exhausted.

She wanted to take a warm shower to ease her aching muscles but there had been no hot water left since Starr had left the water running for who knows how long!

Lying in the dark in her bed, Mary sighs.

She and Starr had been so close as the girl had grown from a child into teenager. Often times she felt like she depended on Starr too much but the girl never complained and seemed so happy with the life they had made for themselves after Travis had left.

But now there is an underlying tension between them that she had no idea how to confront simply because she does not know where it is coming from.

Trying to talk to Starr is like talking to wall these days so that has not yielded any results.

She has been wracking her brain trying to figure out if she had unintentionally done or said something to anger or push her daughter away.

She could not think of anything and lets out another sigh of frustration.

She tosses and turns in the bed, punching her pillow before settling down again. Her eyes still remain wide open in the darkened bedroom.

It is times like this that she wished that she had a man around – to help her deal with things like this. She had been without a partner for so long and she feels drained from trying to be a mother and father on her own.

Travis is hardly ever here and while his words the other night gave the impression that he intended to change that, she could not place false hope on them.

She had after all married this man, thinking their love match would be a happily ever after story only to realize what a fool she had been.

Pierre comes to mind then. After the whole fiasco with him walking in on the two of them having breakfast with Travis, things have been strained.

He did not answered her call for the longest time and when he finally did, their words had been angered.

Still, she missed his company. He helped her fill the lonely hours with laughter and camaraderie.

She glances at the clock. It is very late.

She knows she should not but she wonders if she should call him again nonetheless.

Her walls are down after the weird confrontation she had with Starr and she just needs to talk to someone.

The need pushes her to get out of her bed. She will call Pierre. She walks to the kitchen where one of the phone lines are set up. There are two but lately Starr has been hogging the portable one. Just as she is about to pick up the phone she hears whispering coming from Starr's bedroom and notices the blinking light on the device.

Starr is talking to someone on the phone.

Who is she talking to this late and about what? Mary thinks to herself.

The curiosity and motherly concern is killing her and she knows she has to find out

———— ❧ ————

It is around midnight and Starr cannot sleep.

The events of the day weigh on her mind. Mary has already gone to bed, tired from the day at work.

She had wanted to take a shower but could not because Starr has used up all the hot water, leaving it running for quite a while. She had been further angered by the fact and had let Starr know it. Starr had not been bothered and Mary's words had gone into one ear only to tumble right out the other.

All she can think about is Pierre and the wonderful feelings he incited in her body. She chooses not to focus on her disappointment and hurt after.

She needs to tell someone about what happened and picks up the phone without thinking.

She dials the cell phone number and the phone rings.

After the third ring, her roller coaster of emotion brings her to impatience and frustration.

"Kandy, pick up the damn phone," she growls softly. Finally, a low and sleep-filled voice answers, "Hello?" Whispering, Starr says excitedly, "Guess what, bitch?"

Clearly knowing who is on the line, Kandy sounds more awake when she asks, "What is it, Starr?"

"I have been to heaven and back," she boasts.

"What are you talking about?" Kandy says, sounding annoyed. "And this shit better be good because it is almost 1 AM."

"In the morning," Starr replies. "Pierre did it. *We* did it. And it was marvelous!"

There is a pause as her friend puts the pieces together. Then Kandy goes, "Oh, you tramp! You have got to be lying." Starr starts to giggle and Kandy does too.

Kandy says, "If *she* finds out, your ass is going to be fucked up." Starr is about to respond but she hears a clicking noise indicating someone else is on the line.

"Mom! Mom, I'm on the phone," she yells. "Just hang up."

"Starr, who are you talking to?" Mary asks and it is Kandy who answers the suddenly three-way call.

"Oh, it's just me, Ms. Dixon, Kandy."

"Oh," Mary says. "Well, it's too late for this. You girls should be asleep. You both have a big day tomorrow. You don't want to be falling asleep during your graduation ceremony."

"Yes, Ma'am," Kandy replies demurely.

"Just give me one more minute, Mom," Starr says.

"One more minute," Mary replied then there is another click to indicate that she has exited the call.

"How much do you think she heard, Kandy?" Starr asks, trembling with the adrenaline rush.

Oh no, could Mary have already found out about her sexual encounter with Pierre?

"I don't know, girl but we'd better hang up because she might pick up the line again," replies Kandy.

They hang up and Starr sits in the darkness pondering whether or not she had unwillingly spilled the beans about herself and Pierre having sex to her mother.

CHAPTER THIRTEEN

It is the next morning, 9:30 AM.

It is big day, today. She graduates from high school tonight.

Mary is already out and about and Starr is still in bed, tired from her late night. It took her a very long time to fall asleep, worry causing her insomnia.

She has only just gotten up at Mary's urging. Breakfast is ready. It is time to face the music and find out if her affair with Pierre has been found out.

She drags herself out of bed and goes into the kitchen, afraid of the reaction she will get from Mary.

They have not seen each other at all yet and she is unsure of what reaction she will get from her mother. Plus, she does not know if she can look her mother in the eyes since her feelings of guilt have resurfaced.

She enters the kitchen and finds Mary at the stove. Mary is dressed in her pajamas still, full-length pants and a tank top that make her look like a teenager herself.

Mary does not look up form what she is doing but when she hears Starr enter the room, she says, "Your father called and asked about the graduation. He is flying in today, he says. He will be there to see you complete school."

Still in a daze, Starr can only muster a reply of, "Ahuh."

Her lackluster tone pulls Mary's attention to her and she holds her breath, half expecting a blowout then.

Mary's eyes look her over before Mary shakes her head and goes back to what she is doing.

"I told you you should not have stayed up so late last night," is all Mary says, clearly thinking all that is the matter is Starr's lack of a good night's sleep.

Phew, Starr thinks. It looks like she and Pierre had not been caught but she still she remains vigilant all day, looking for clues otherwise.

Mary took the day off work and helps Starr prepare for the evening's event. This time Starr is dressed in a neutral black dress that reaches her knees and black pumps with red soles. She looks beautiful with her hair dropped and straightened and her sedate makeup makes her look so very grown up.

Pierre is not at the house this time, his estrangement from Mary very apparent. Mary had given Starr a half-assed excuse as to why he was absent but she knows better.

Starr misses him and has to talk herself out of calling him several times. She doesn't know if she can handle his response to her if it is anything other than thrilled to hear from her. She just may go crazy after all that happened the day before.

Besides, she has hardly had a minute to herself with Mary hovering so close so often while the two get prepared to go. The phone has been ringing on and off all evening but with all the hustle and bustle neither of them has time to answer it. Eventually, the two women leave the house with things still strained between them but both wearing fake bright smiles.

After the graduation ceremony, Mary hangs back to talk with a few of the other parents while Starr goes to the entrance of the hall, ready to leave.

She looks every bit the successful graduate with her gown covering her dress and diploma in hand but she does not feel happy like she should.

Her mind is elsewhere… On Pierre, actually.

Even though things are strange between Pierre and her mother, she still expected him to show up for her big day. Seeing as she has not caught a glimpse of him anywhere, she just wants to go home and throw herself a pity party in her bedroom.

She distantly realizes that she has not seen Travis even though Mary said he would be here.

Oh well, she thinks. It is not like she is surprised by his no-show. Still, she puts on happy face as she takes pictures with her friends and classmates. Her smile only drops a little when she notices Kandy whisper something to Yvette while the two look over in her direction.

The judgmental look on Yvette's face lets her know exactly what the two are talking about.

Whatever, she thinks, turning her back on them. *Jealous bitches.* Just then a stretched limousine pulls up in front of the building. "Starr" is written across the long, white surface.

There is silence as the persons who are outside look from the luxury vehicle to Starr.

She moves closer to the car, her heart beating faster with each step.

The driver steps out with a huge bouquet of red roses. He is a slim dark-skinned man dressed formally in a black suit and black cap.

He comes up to her and says, "Are you Miss Starr?" "Yes, I am," she replies, already feeling breathless with anticipation.

"I have specific orders to pick you up and bring you someplace very special. Someone who adores you sent me. Will you come with me?" he asks.

A huge smile breaks out across Starr's face at her idea of who this person who adores her is.

She takes a look back and sees the excited, the shocked and best of all, the envious looks of some of the people in the crowd gathering around the limo.

She spots her mother exiting the building in a hurry. Mary is coming toward Starr with a worried look on her face.

"Starr," Mary calls.

"I'll be back soon, Mom," she yells and waves. Turning back to the driver, she says, "Alright, take me to "this person who adores" me. Hurry."

He holds the door open for her and she quickly enters the car before her mother reaches her. The drivers takes off before Mary breaks through the crowd.

As the school hall disappears in the distance she goes up to the windows dividing the front and back of the limo and says to the driver, "Sir, who sent you?"

He does not look back but meets her eyes in the rearview mirror and says, "My instructions are not to tell you. It is a surprise. Sit back and enjoy the ride."

Starr does as instructed and soon the limo pulls up to a fancy hotel way across town.

There is a man standing at the curb and she recognizes the figure instantly.

Pierre.

He has a tuxedo on.

He opens the door for her and helps her out. She barely notices that the limo is driven away after she exits.

She does not have a chance to say anything because Pierre grabs her and kisses her passionately.

When he lets her go, she has to catch her breath before saying, "Why did you do this?"

He tells her, "I want to make your graduation night special. I have gown waiting for you so we can have our own party."

That sounds lovely and special but something weighs on Starr's mind.

"Why did you leave me yesterday?" she asks, searching his face. Pierre takes a deep breath and replied, "The way I feels about you scared me, it is so strong. I think I am falling in love with you.

I'm sorry, baby. Forgive me?"

He looks so sincere and she loves him so much that she could not help saying, "I forgive you. I am falling in love with you, too." That is a lie. She has already fallen so deep but something keeps her from confessing the depth of her feelings just yet.

They share another kiss before going to a hotel room with a breathtaking view of the city. Starr takes a quick shower and changes into the gown Pierre has laid out for her. It is a deep red color and fits her like a glove, highlighting her every curve.

Pierre has another surprise waiting for her. There is a talent young makeup artist and hairstylist there to do her makeup and hair.

When all the pampering and styling has been done, Starr looks and feels like a princess.

Pierre takes her hand and leads her down to the hotel's ballroom. They dance for more than two hours then have a grand dinner. Pierre is mentally seducing Starr and her body is begging to be seduced too.

Finally, he takes her back to the room.

There are candles lit and rose petals are everywhere. The lights are dim and slow music is playing.

Pierre closes the door behind them and pulls her body close to his.

His starts making love to her slow and soon her pretty dress is pooled around her ankles. He takes his time to kiss every inch of her nubile body and she lets out pleasure-filled sighs and moans.

She is completely naked when she feels him take away his mouth. She opens her eyes to find him holding out a bright red piece of lingerie.

"Here, put this on, baby," he says and of course, she will do anything he commands.

A few minutes later, she comes out of the bathroom, clothed in the sexy piece of lace and satin.

Pierre has undressed and is waiting for her on the bed. He beckons her closer and she goes without hesitation.

He seduces her and leaves her feeling on top of the world. No one else matters but the two of them.

CHAPTER FOURTEEN

Mary is at home pacing the floor and wondering where her daughter is.

Who sent that limo? she wonders.

Why did Starr take off like that? Without even a word of explanation?

She sighs deeply, tapping her fingers against her thighs as she walks around the kitchen table.

She had even resorted to calling Starr's girlfriends, hoping for a clue as to where Starr went but they do not know either. They all sounded strange on the phone and she has to wonder if they are lying to her.

But why would they? She has known all these girls since they were in diapers and they have never been so closed off from her before. Why now?

It is already after midnight when the phone rings. Mary rushes to it and answers, "Hello?"

A male voice says, "I'm sorry I called so late but I am hoping I can speak to my little graduate even though it is late. I wanted to make it up there time to see the ceremony but my flight got delayed. I tried calling you guys a few times today but there was no answer."

"Oh Travis, it's you. How are you?" Mary says, leaning against the wall. Her emotions are whirling inside her and she is tired from the weight of them.

"I'm fine, Mary, but you don't sound so good. Are you and Starr okay?" Travis asks.

She cannot help but unload the drama with Starr going MIA act tonight.

"I am sure that she is fine though. She is a very smart young lady and I am confident that she is not making decisions that will put her in any danger," she ends, trying to convince herself. "But I don't like that she just took off like that without a word to me. I feel like I am losing my little girl and I have no idea how to stop it, you know."

"Do you think she will return home tonight?" he asks her.

"I can't tell you. She is so unpredictable these days. But she is eighteen now. I cannot dictate her coming and going now." Again, Mary sighs.

"I'm staying at a friend's house not too far from you guys until I settle things with my own apartment. Do you mind if I stop by? I can keep you company until Starr gets home. I know you won't sleep a wink until she does," Travis offers.

"I would love that," she says, genuinely happy to not be alone right now.

Pierre is still giving her the cold shoulder and has not answered the call she placed to him earlier that night.

"I'll see you soon," Travis says and hangs up.

About fifteen minutes later, there is a knock on the door. "Who is it?" Mary calls.

"Guess who?" a male voice teases from the other side of the door.

She knows that voice. Travis.

She opens the door to reveal this buff figure. He blocks of the night and the rest of the world. It is almost like they are the only ones who exist.

They stand there looking at one another for a moment before she snaps out of her daze and says, "Come in, Travis."

The door closes and the two share a brief hug.

Mary ignores the tingly feelings she gets feeling his hard body and smelling his unique male scent.

She puts on some coffee and the two keep each other company. Starr is not far from her mind but she begins to unwind with her ex-husband.

They are sitting in the living room much later – around 4 AM to be exact - when he says, "Mary, when I left your life eleven years ago, I knew you that you were a quality woman with the potential to be whatever you wanted. Any man would be lucky to have you. I guess want I'm really getting at is, do you have another man in your life? I mean, I get that there is something between and that guy that showed up the other day but is it serious?"

Mary feels like she is on shaky ground. On one hand, she is happy that he is clearly still interested in her even though she knows she should not be. On the other hand, she is nervous and a bit embarrass to confess, "Well, there has only been one man since you left."

"Only one?" Travis seems amazed. "That guy? Pierre?"

"Yeah," Mary answers. "It's been about five years since he's been coming around."

"Are you guys living together?" He leans toward her as he asks. He is so close, she can see the specks of gold in his warm brown eyes. The scent of his cologne is wrapping around her and making it hard to think.

She tells him, "No."

"Why not?" he continues to probe.

She hesitates, ashamed of the truth. "Well, Travis, Pierre is married."

He pauses and she watches closely for his reaction. She expects condemnation but his expression is completely closed when he says, "Oh, I see."

There is another pause then he looks into her eyes and says, "I want you back, Mary and I know this Pierre does not deserve you. The fact that he is in your life will not stop me from trying to make you mine again. I want you and my daughter back. I want us to be a family again."

She does not have time to feel the shock of his words because his lips are on hers and all she can do is feel.

CHAPTER FIFTEEN

It is Friday night.

Almost a whole week has passed since Starr's graduation.

Friday is usually Mary and Pierre's date night and unexpectedly he called her the day before to confirm that they are still on.

She should be on cloud nine that he seems to want to work things out now but her thoughts are barely on him even as she gets ready for the date.

Mary is feeling guilty. She slept with Travis the night of Starr's graduation.

He claims to still be in love with her and while her heart is glad to hear that, her head is telling her she would be a fool to believe anything he has to say. He claimed to love her once before only to leave her high and dry.

The doorbell rings and Starr shouts from the living room, "I'll get it."

"Okay," Mary answers. "If it's Pierre, tell him to come back here." The relationship between Mary and her daughter has not improved at all since Starr's disappearing act. In fact, things are worse now.

Starr had shown up the day after graduation around 9 AM. The limo had dropped her on the curb and sped off before Mary could confront the driver. By then, Travis had already left, needing to get to work.

Trying to get answers out of Starr proved to be impossible. She shuts down every time Mary inquires about where she came from and that only leads to a fight between the two of them.

Mary is worried about her daughter more than ever now and the dreamy smile she often wears when she thinks Mary is not watching is not helping decrease the emotion one bit.

"Hello, beautiful," Pierre greets Starr with a huge smile as she opens up the door for him.

He gives a hot look up and down and she gets tingly all over, remembering the ways he has made love to her these past few days.

They have seen each other every night since he secreted her away to that hotel room… until two days ago.

She used to sneak out of the house after Mary had gone to sleep and he drives them to a hotel where they, of course, spend the night making love passionately.

She is utterly and obsessively in love with this man and cannot be happier. That is until he pissed her off.

"I've been calling you for two days and you have not responded," she tells him coldly, coming at him with a major attitude. "What? Now that we have had sex, are you giving me the cold shoulder?" "Shhh, your mother might hear you," he says, looking in the direction of Mary's bedroom where she is still getting ready so they can go to a movie.

And that is another thing to add to her ire. Starr cannot believe that Pierre is following through with their date night! She thought he would end things with Mary after he found Travis here and thought they were messing around. Why has he not broken up with her mother?

Irked even more now, she crosses her arms, leans toward him and threatens, "If you're avoiding me, I will make our relationship public."

"I'm not! I'm not, Starr! Just chill. I've been with my wife. She is beginning to get suspicious because I have not been around much as lately. It was not so bad when I was just seeing your mother but I have been seeing you a lot more and she noticed that routine has switched up."

He does not get to say anymore because Mary walks into the den just then.

"Why didn't you send Pierre to the back like I asked you to, Starr?"

Starr rolls her eyes at her mother and walks to her bedroom. She slams the door shut.

⚬⚬⚬

Mary flinches at the violent sound of the door slamming.

She turns to Pierre and asks, "What's wrong with her? What is she mad about now? What did you say to her?"

She notices a light sweat on his brown before he answers, "Oh babe, she is just pissed that I still have not taken her to that graduation dinner at that fancy restaurant on the west side of town that I promised her."

Mary goes, "Oh, okay. You promised to take her to a fancy restaurant for dinner?"

This is the first she is hearing about this.

"Yeah, I promised as a graduation present since I missed the ceremony."

"Alright," Mary says, telling herself that it is not big deal.

"We should get going," Pierre says and Mary begins gathering her things for them to leave.

Before they can exit the house though Starr storms back out of her bedroom and demands, "So when are you guys coming back?"

Taken aback by Starr's aggression, Mary says, "I don't know. Why?"

"Because the movie should be over by 11 PM," Starr says.

Her frustration bubbles to the top and Mary tells her daughter, "Look, I don't know what your problem is but you need to watch your tone, missy. I am tired of this rotten attitude of yours." "Whatever," is Starr's response and shortly after she slams her bedroom door shut again.

Sighing, Mary turns to Pierre and says, "Come on, baby, let's get out of here."

The two leave shortly after.

⸺⁓⁓⸺

Starr is steaming mad after she hears the front door close.

She knows that she is acting jealous and possessive and does nothing to curb her actions because that is exactly how she feels. There is the possibility that Mary and Pierre might have sex if they stay out too late.

She cannot allow that to happen. She just cannot.

CHAPTER SIXTEEN

At the theatre, about halfway through the movie, Pierre's cell phone rings yet again. The device is in his pants pocket and no doubt Mary can feel them too.

It is confirmed when she leans close to him and whispers, "Do you need to get that?"

He pulls the phone out of his pocket and looks at the caller ID discreetly. It stops ringing while in his hand.

"Uh," he says irritability. "That's my wife. I'll be right back." Mary nods, not paying him much attention as she watches the chick flick. Pierre gets out of his seat and walks out of the room. He goes out into the hall and returns the call.

"Starr, what's up? Why do you keep on calling me?"

He has been trying to pull back from Starr as of late because she is acting very clingy and demanding more and more of his time. He should have completely cut her off he knows, but she is a physical temptation he just cannot resist.

She immediately goes in on him. "When are you guys going to leave the movies? And when are you going to leave *her* alone?" Pierre rubs a hand over his face. "I don't know."

The attitude come across the line when she answers, "Well, you had better start knowing. I'm the one who is supposed to be with you, not her."

Pierre is getting angry now. He will not have an immature girl like this tell him what to do.

"You need to watch your temper, miss," he tells Starr. "Because you're going to give us up. You know I care for you, baby, and I'm missing you a lot but you have to be patient. Things will be just as you want them all in due time."

He knows immediately that his words had the desired calming effect.

"You miss me?" she asks, all soft and feminine now.

"I do, baby," he replies, injecting the hot lust that he feels for her in his tone. "I will see you later."

"Okay," she says.

He hangs up and goes back in to finish watching the movie with the unsuspecting Mary.

About an hour later, they are leaving the theatre when he gets a call from his wife for real this time.

He does not answer until he and Mary are settled in his SUV. "Hey, I missed your call. I was just pumping gas. Did you call me?" he asks Karen.

She goes on, "Yes, I did. We need to talk."

Her tone disturbs him but he dismisses the feeling.

"Okay, honey. I'll be there soon," he tells her and hangs up.

He drives Mary home and they get very cozy in the driveway. She reaches for him and he does not resist. They begin kissing fiercely. He gets a thrill being close to this woman even though he has been intimate with her daughter.

———⸙———

Starr is peeking out the window and sees them in the act of kissing.

She is furious.

Her earlier good mood is completely gone and a jealous rage fills her.

———⸙———

Pierre notices a curtain move inside and knows Starr is peeking in on him and Mary.

No doubt he will feel her wrath soon.

Still, he takes his time pulling away from Mary.

Her eyes look into his and she says, "I had a great time." "I did as well," he tells her.

"I know things have been strained between us lately. I am hoping that we can get past that," she goes on to say.

"Me too. I overreacted the other day. Forgive me?" he puts on his best puppy dog face and she laughs.

"Of course, I do," she says easily. "I'd better go in now." She gets out and goes inside.

He drives off.

He heads home but luckily Karen is already asleep when he arrives.

After a pause, he turns around and leaves the house.

———⸙———

Where the hell is he going? He promised to be with me when he left my mother.

Starr is fuming as he watches Pierre's tail lights disappear.

She is certainly not in any mood to entertain her mother when Mary seeks her out to ask, "What is the matter with you?" She turns her back on Mary and says, "Nothing."

Later, she is lying in her bed in the dark when her cell phone beeps. The device was a gift from Pierre on the night of her graduation.

It is a text from him.

I'm waiting from you in the driveway.

She watches the words for many seconds, wanting to ignore him out of spite but she cannot not.

She loves him too much to.

Sneaking out is easy since Mary is already asleep.

A few minutes later, she enters Pierre's SUV. He pulls away from Mary's home and heads in the direction of the hotel they usually stayed at.

It is quiet for a little while and she angles her body away from him, clearly conveying that she is still displeased with him. That attitude melts away when he starts saying the things she wants to hear like how beautiful she is and soon it will be just the two of them.

They are almost naked by the time they reach the room.

The door closes behind them.

Back at home, Mary is on the phone with Travis.

She is laying in her bed, in her nightclothes and thinks that her daughter is already asleep at this late hour. She went to bed a long time ago but has not been able to fall asleep.

"I really enjoyed myself the other night," he tells her.

She feels her face heat up in the memory of making love to him. He knew how to push her buttons like no other man when they were younger and he still does even now.

"I enjoyed myself too," she replies softly.

"I hope we can pick up where we left off. I truly do regret leaving you and my baby girl. I want to show you more than ever I can be the man that you need," he tells in a similarly low voice.

"Things are complicated with me and Pierre right now but we will see," she tells him vaguely.

She moves the conversation away from getting back together and brings up their daughter.

The two are talking about Starr's behavior and she tells him what happened earlier that night.

Suddenly Travis says, "Do you think she is attracted to Pierre?" Mary's heart stops in her chest but quickly picks up again when she sucks her teeth and laughs. The idea is totally preposterous. "No Travis, don't be stupid," she says.

"Do you think he is attracted to Starr?" Travis presses.

Mary is getting annoyed with these implications and tells him as much.

"No, Travis. Stop with these questions. You're beginning to piss me off."

They had begun their conversation on a good note when he called but as they hang up, things had definitely turned sour.

Mary settles into bed but cannot sleep still, her mind repeatedly coming back to Travis's questions about Starr and Pierre.

She never in a million years wants to believe that her daughter and her lover would be attracted to each other.

Pierre lets Starr go to get the Jacuzzi going and to dim the lights. There is wine and tasty little chocolate treats.

All the shit from the last few days melt away from Starr's mind. Her dress is a heap on the floor when he picks her up in his strong arms and carries her to the Jacuzzi. He kisses her madly before gently settling her in the water.

He gets in too, naked, and gets under the water to please her. She is in bliss, totally.

She always is when it is just the two of them.

Eventually, she will figure out how to make so that it is just the two of them.

She is tired of sharing her man with two other women.

She is determined to show him that she is the only woman he needs.

When she is lax with pleasure, Pierre takes her out of the water and carries her to the bed, laying her glistening body on the soft sheets.

Their lovemaking is slow and gentle and Starr feels consumed by this man. The way he looks at her, she is certain he feels this all-consuming passion too. He cannot possibly not.

As he penetrates her welcoming body she looks to the side and notices the silhouette of him taking her. She looks higher and for the first time notices a mirror on the ceiling.

They are moving and her head is going back and forth. She smiles to herself. She sees the look of total devotion on Pierre's face too and she knows that they both having the time of their lives.

They make love over and over again until the sun comes up and only then do they fall into an exhausted sleep.

CHAPTER SEVENTEEN

It is 10AM when Starr and Pierre awake.

Only two days have passed and Starr had left the house with the excuse to her mother that she was spending the night at Alyssa's. She and Pierre had spent the night at the usual hotel.

Starr looks at her cell phone. She has one missed call from her mother and many more from Travis.

Pierre grabs his cell phone and sees that Karen has called once as well.

He tells Starr, "I need to call her back. I need you to be quiet while I do this."

Starr looks at him, anger settling over her face before she gets up, goes to the bathroom and slams the door shut.

When his wife answers his call, Pierre lies, "Oh hey, baby. My phone was dead. Was there anything that you wanted?"

There is a pause before she answers, "Never mind, I already got it."

She hangs up on him.

He frowns at the dial tone in his ear, a little concerned but he is happy that the call was short with Starr being so close by. She might have blurted something out and given them away. He never knows with her unpredictable nature.

No sooner does he have the thought, she comes out of the bathroom, clothed and says, "Take me home."

He gets off the bed, still naked and goes to kiss her.

"Okay, baby," he says, using his sexiest voice because he knows that she is mad.

She turns her head away from his kiss. "Just take me home," she insists.

"I just needed to see what she wanted, Starr. It's no big deal. Come on, don't be like that."

He tries to coax her out of her bad mood but she only repeats, "Now, Pierre. I want to go home."

"Fine, I need to drop you off before you mother notices anything anyway," he says, giving up.

"Hurry," she tells him. Rolling her eyes, she leaves him to get dressed.

She is waiting for him in the vehicle and he drives her home. They do not say a word to each other and she jumps out without a goodbye as soon as he pulls up about a block away.

Mary is at home this morning and they are making sure she does not catch them.

A little pissed off too now, Pierre takes off with a loud screech of tires.

A few minutes later, he is cooled off and now thinking he needs to do some damage control with Starr.

He does not want her mad at him. He is already missing the tight hold of her body even though he should be worn out after the night before.

When Starr enters the home, Mary calls, "Starr is that you?"

"Yes, it's me. I'm going to my room," she answers.

She does not want to see her mother right now. She is likely to say or do something very bad.

Not too long after her door closes behind her.

She hears Mary make an exasperated sound but does not care. She has undressed and freshened up when Pierre calls her cell phone.

She picks up and he tells her how much he enjoyed himself last night and how he hates how they left things.

She cannot stay mad at him and says, "I'm sorry. I was being childish and overreacted. I blew things out of proportion. I just hate not having you all to myself."

"All in due time, baby," he says.

"I don't want to wait. I want you now," she stresses.

"It's not like we can just get rid of your mother, you know," he tells her.

"Why not?" Starr asks without thinking. "I will do anything to be with you. I can get a gun you know. I'm eighteen now."

There is a shocked silence on the other end of the line and after the words have come out, Starr feels a little shocked at herself too.

But not enough to regret or take back her words.

"I can just kill her," she says and the words are more to herself than to Pierre as her mind races a mile a minute as it sees this new way to get all that she wants.

There is more silence but then Pierre shocks her by saying, "That will be too messy though. You cannot just blow her brains out when she comes home from work. Forensics would have a field day with that. I don't know if we should do it like that. We can poison her but the she might suffer and I know you don't want to see her suffer."

"I don't care about her. All I care about is us," she says. Then she wonders, "But what about your wife? We're talking about getting rid of my mom but you're still married."

Pierre makes a careless sound and answers, "I can leave her." Starr frowns. "But we can't kill my mom and keep her around. Why should we?"

Pierre says, "Because there is my child. She needs someone there with her every day."

"Okay," Starr concedes. "You have a point. I'll think of a way that we do this. Until then, when can I see you again, Daddy?

She adds the last part to be teasing but likes the sound of it on her lips referring to him.

Pierre laughs and says, "Soon, sweetheart. Really soon." They hang up.

Starr lays on the bed, plans already forming in her head. Finally, she has found a way for her to get all she wants and be happy.

CHAPTER EIGHTEEN

The very next day, Starr is out with Alyssa.

Initially, she had invited Alyssa along with her to go to the mall and they had stopped at the food court. It is there she dropped her bomb.

Today, she is going to buy a gun… and she wants Alyssa to tag along with her to the gun shop.

Of course, she had not been truthful with Alyssa about why she wants to buy the weapon.

She made up a story about want to feel secure and protected because someone has been making obscene phone calls to the house to her and Mary.

"It's probably just someone playing games, Starr," had been Alyssa's response. "You cannot buy a gun for something silly like that."

"Well, it's just my mother and I, and there is no one around to protect us," Starr said.

"Still, don't you think buying a guy is a little too much," Alyssa had said.

"It's just in case there is an emergency. It's not like I plan to kill anyone, Alyssa," Starr had said with a laugh.

Alyssa had joined her and said, "Right. I guess I see why you would want to get one."

And that is how they ended by at this gun store a few blocks from the mall.

The sales associate, a thin, Caucasian guy named Gary, is eager to show Starr and Alyssa their options.

As soon as he shows Starr a three fifty-seven though, she does not need to see anything else.

She takes it from him and caresses the small, handgun.

Wow, this can really do the job well, she thinks, sinking deeper and deeper into her mind where all her devious plans lie.

She glances up to find Alyssa looking at her very strangely and now, she wonders why she even bothered bringing the other girl along.

"What are you talking about?" Alyssa asks her.

"What do you mean? I did not say anything," Starr replies, frowning.

"Yes, you did. You said, "This can do the job well", is Alyssa's response, which makes Starr realize that she had spoken out loud.

"No, I didn't," Starr denies. "You must be hearing things, 'Lyssa." She laughs as if Alyssa is being absurd. She turns to the sale associate who gives her some paperwork to fill out when she tells him that she will take the three fifty-seven. He informs her that a background check need to be done.

When all the preliminaries are done, he let her know that she has to wait three business days before she can find out whether or not she is approved to purchase the weapon.

"Okay," Starr says, feeling very happy that she has taken this first step in making her life go the way she wants it to.

She and Alyssa leave the shop.

Alyssa drives Starr home in her small car but the two barely speak. The fact does not bother Starr. She does not want to talk to the girl either.

In fact, she is feeling that she needs to rethink the so-called friendships she has in her life.

She gets out when Alyssa stops in her driveway.

She throws a careless, "Bye" in Alyssa's direction and does not look back as she enters the house.

Across town, Travis has taken it upon himself to start investigating Pierre and his involvement with Starr.

Starr has been avoiding him, barely answering his calls. And her behavior toward Mary is becoming more and more out of hand. He knows that he has not been around much and that Mary is more than likely a better judge of Starr's character and moods than he but he does not buy that she is just going through a teenage girl's mood swing.

It is more than that and he knows that it revolves around Mary's adulterous boyfriend, Pierre.

The way that man looked at his daughter during the confrontation they had when Travis just came into town has Travis suspicion.

That was the look of a man real familiar with a woman. And the look Starr gave him has Travis even more worried. Her eyes were those of a woman in love and they were pointed at the man in Mary's life.

No matter what Mary says, he knows that something is going on between Pierre and Starr.

He just has to find out what and he plans to find out sooner rather than later.

CHAPTER NINETEEN

Back at Pierre's home, he has finally sat down to have that talk he promised his wife.

They are seated at the island of their huge eat-in kitchen and only inches from each other.

Karen in dressed in a summer dress that falls to her knees and a pair of black sandals. Her hair is done up into a sophisticated updo that makes her cheekbones look more prominent and the line of her neck look long and graceful.

Sophisticated and graceful are great words to describe his wife. Such a contrast to Starr's untamed gorgeousness. Once, he was the talk of the town having Karen on his arm, such a beautiful woman from a well-known family. Now they are just another couple with nothing exciting going on.

He wondered what would happen if he shown up with Starr, a bombshell in her own right, on his arm at one of the charity event Karen loves to drag him to. There would be talk, he knows and he damn sure knows that he would be the envy of the men there accompanied by lovely, sophisticated wives just like Karen. They would love to be him with such an obviously sexual and hot young woman looking up at him with absolute devotion in her eyes.

Karen is watching him so he pushes thoughts of his forbidden affair to the side before he outs himself.

Despite being unhappy with Karen there is no denying that his marriage to her has taken him away from a hard life and into the fast lane. Without her name and family backing, he would not be where he is today – a well-respected family man living in a prominent neighborhood with a great job in a senator's office that still has lots of upward mobility.

There is no way he is giving that up for a piece of tail, no matter how great it is.

When she delivers her news though, the panic in his chest makes him wish he had avoid this talk for longer.

"I'm pregnant."

She looks him dead in the eye as she says this and he has to hide his reaction under a mask of mild surprise and shock. Really, he is hiding the urge to run out the door in terror.

"Are you sure?" he asks her carefully.

"Of course, I am positive," Karen replies, composure in place while he is trying not to break out into a sweat. "I would not have come to you with this unless I was. I am four months along. We conceive the last time we were together physically."

"O-Okay," he stammers, trying to find the right response to this. She sighs as he mentally scrambles for a way to handle this and looks away briefly before looking at him again.

"What I want to know is, are you going to be here for me and our unborn child?" she asks.

He scrunches his brow and puts a look of confusion on his face.

"Of course! Why would you say a thing like that?" he cries, aghast.

"Well, you have not been here for me lately and I thought it is because you want out of this marriage," she says, completely straight-faced until the last word. Then her façade cracks and she begins to cry.

"No! No, baby. I have working double shifts trying to make a better living for you and our little girl, that's all," he tells her leaning close.

Something flashes in her eyes before she shifts her gaze away from his.

"Stop lying to me, Pierre. Just stop."

She tells him this, voice breaking. Then she gets up and walks out on him.

When she disappears, he rubs a hand over his head and face and long minutes pass with him in that position.

Then he pulls out his phone and his finger hovers over Starr's name.

He *needs* to see her.

Before he sends the call, he stops himself.

He cannot leave Karen alone now. It will be too obvious. *Later*, he promises himself and gets up to go try to salvage his marriage.

Mary is asleep when Pierre calls Starr.

Starr presses a button on the cell to record their conversation as soon as the call connects. It is something she has taken up doing so she can play their calls back and listen to his voice when he is not around.

"I need to see you," he tells her. "How about I come pick you up and we go somewhere private?"

Having fun with this conversation, Starr leans back in her bed, twirling her hair in her fingers and smiling at the ceiling. She is dressed in pajama shorts and a small top. Her bare feet kick at the air in her joy at hearing from him even though they spoke earlier that day.

"Well, how bad do you want to see me?" she teases.

"Really bad, baby," he does not hesitate to say and she melts under the need in his voice. Her body responds immediately and she squirms where she lays.

"Okay, come get me," she gives him her permission.

"Great. I'm waiting for you in the driveway. Wear something sexy and come outside," he replies.

"Presumptuous, aren't you?" she says even though she is already off her bed and searching for that sexy outfit.

"No, I just know my woman needs me as much as I need her," he says and she falls that much deeper for this man.

"I'll be right there," she says and they hang up.

He takes her to a hotel and they spend the night sexing before he drops her back in her driveway before the sun or her mother gets up.

CHAPTER TWENTY

The next morning, Starr is up bright and early and in a great mood despite the lack of sleep the previous night.

Mary is up and about, getting ready for work. Starr can hear her bustling about as she lays in bed reminiscing about the night before.

There is a knock at the door and it is Pierre.

Starr hears his voice and quickly gets out of bed. She rushes to the front of the house, eager to see him only to stop short. Mary has already opened up the door for Pierre and the two are standing in the kitchen. She goes against the hallway wall and peeks around the corner, eavesdropping on their conversation. She confirms neither one of them has seen her yet when they start talking.

Pierre has a huge bouquet of flowers which he hands to Mary and says, "Hi, baby."

Mary is as surprised by his visit as Starr is and asks "What are you doing here?"

"Why are you so surprised to see me? I told you I want us to make things up. I was out of line when I saw Travis here and I *am* sorry. You know I love you, right?"

Starr's good mood vanishes. She is furious now. Absolutely fuming. She wants to run up to Pierre and start hitting him. But she does not. There is a cold edge to her anger that curbs the impulse and she stands back and continues to watch.

Mary and Pierre embrace and he continues to say, "My jealousy just got the best of me. I saw Starr's father here and I just assumed that you guys were back together. I thought that you were sneaking around behind my back and I was hurt so I lashed out."

Mary cups his cheek and says, "Oh Pierre, you don't need to worry about Travis."

By this time, Starr has had enough and storms into the kitchen. Pierre's eyes widen as he sees her and her clear anger. He probably thought she would still be asleep and not witness this little tete-a-tete between him and Mary.

He breaks away from Mary and Mary sees Starr. Mary frowns, sensing Starr foul mood.

Starr faces her mother and goes, "Did you at least cook breakfast?"

Mary steps back, clearly taken aback by this aggression.

"Uh, no," she answers. "I didn't cook today. And good morning to you too, Starr."

Ignoring the chiding in her mother's words and tone, Starr turns her gaze to Pierre and stares at him.

He looks down, around, everywhere but at her. He turns his gaze to Mary, who Starr can see watching her.

Mary finally breaks the awkward silence that follows and says, "Stop being rude, Starr. Say good morning to Pierre."

Instead of doing what her mother says, she walks away. She goes to her bedroom and slams the door.

I can't wait until I get my gun, she thinks, red hot with her fury.

Mary turns to Pierre, embarrassed and upset about Starr's outburst.

"That girl," she starts. "I don't know what is wrong with her but she needs to stop acting out like this. I don't know what is going on with her. I thought it was a phase but it is more than that apparently."

Pierre nods his head, brow marked with concern as he glances in the direction of Starr's bedroom.

"Let me talk to her while you finish getting ready for work," he offers.

"Maybe her dad being back around is making her feel some type of way," Mary musses out loud but knows that is not it. Starr has been acting out long before Travis showed up in the picture again. "I really don't know what it is."

"I'll take care of her," Pierre says, already heading in the direction of Starr's bedroom. "I've known her since she was a little girl. I'm pretty sure I can get whatever that is bothering her out of her."

He disappears around the corner and Mary hears him knock on Starr's door.

Even though, Travis' words about the odd relationship between Pierre and Starr echo loudly in her head, she forces her feet to go in the other direction.

"Starr?"

Starr hears Pierre call her from the other side of the door and rolls her eyes.

"What do you want?" she yells.

"Can I come in and talk to you?" he asks.

Her heart skips a beat thinking about him coming close to her even though she is mad. Mary will be gone soon and there will be no one around. They will not need to pretend.

"Whatever," she returns.

Pierre comes in and leaves the door open.

He steps inside and with a huff, she gets up from where she was sitting on the bed and closes the door. She is about to let him have it and she knows he prefers that they do not have an audience when that happens.

"What are you do here?" she says in a hybrid of a shout and a whisper. "Why were you like that with my mom? I thought you were done with her. You know she is fucking my dad no matter what she says. What are doing? You told me you love me."

Even with her tirade, she goes close and tries to kiss on him to show him what incredible chemistry they have. He cannot deny that. All she has to do is make him see and he will stop messing around with Mary.

He pushes her away.

"Keep it down," he hisses at her from between clenched teeth. "You're going to give us up. I only did that so she will not think anything of it when I stop by so that we can spend time together. Plus, I really was rude and out of place for treating them like that when I barged in the other day. It's not my place to tell her who she can and cannot date. Just stop getting on like this. Chill out already."

Starr goes, "No, no! I can't do this. I want you to myself and I can't stand seeing you with her."

She goes back up to him, ignoring his pushing hands and tries to kiss him again.

She sees him weakening, especially when she presses her body against him. His mouth hovers over hers like he is going to kiss her. Just when she thinks she has gotten through to him, the door opens.

Mary comes in and says, "Why is the door shut?"

With his hands on her shoulders, Pierre shakes Starr gently and says, "Starr, you've got to stop being rude to your parents."

His eyes implore her not to give them up and she curses herself for being so weak for this man.

Still, she plays along and goes, "I know, okay."

He continues, "That's not good. You know, I've been around for awhile. I love you like you're my own. You do know I love you, right?"

She blossoms under the word love. "I know you love me, Pierre."

They turn to Mary who is looking between them with wide eyes. Starr goes up to and hugs Mary, laying it on thick. When she pulls back, Mary is smiling and looking hopeful.

Her watches beeps and Mary says, "Oh, I'm going to be late for work. I'm going now."

Outside, Mary starts her car but sits in the driveway for the longest while.

Although she is happy that there has been some sort of breakthrough with Starr, she cannot stop the question that keeps on buzzing around in her head.

Why was the door shut?

She shakes her head and her internal dialogue continues.

My mind is playing tricks on me. Let me stop.

Resolute, she pulls out of the driveway and heads for work.

She does this, leaving her boyfriend her and her daughter alone in the house.

Inside, Pierre is seducing Starr.

They are on the bed and she is naked. He is on top of her and kissing her smooth skin.

Her phone rings and she sees Travis's name pop up on the screen.

Answering his call is definitely not important enough to stop this sensual play between she and Pierre so she ignores it.

There are more calls in the hours that Pierre spends over with Starr, making love in her bed in her mother's home. At one point they knock the device over as things get rougher.

Much later, Pierre gets up and gets dressed.

"Okay, baby. I need to go now. I need to start my day," he says. "And one more thing. You really should be nicer to your mother." Starr had been relaxing back in the tangled sheets, well-satisfied and enjoying herself watching him dress. Now, she is tense, frustration penetrating her afterglow.

She sits up and asks, "Why are you taking up for her?" "There is a way that you should handle things so that we can have a future together and lashing out at your mother all the time is not it."

He leans over to kiss while he says this then adds, "For me, be nice to her."

"Okay, I'll be nice," she tells him.

For him.

He digs into his pocket and hands her a handful of bills, the majority hundreds and says, "Bring her out to lunch to make it up with her."

Shortly after, Pierre is at the front door. Starr kisses him goodbye and he leaves.

She tidies up herself and her bedroom and notices her phone on the floor. She picks it up and scrolls through it.

She sees Kandy's name and minutes used up on an incoming call only minutes ago. The call had been connected for almost thirty minutes.

She immediately calls the other girl back.

Kandy picks after one ring and as a way of greeting says, "Who did you have over there, you tramp? I called and the phone picked up, by accident I'm guessing. I heard you guys fucking like rabbits."

Starr laughs and says slyly, "My man was definitely here." "Well, you picked up my call by accident so you'd better hope your parents had not called and the same thing happened," Kandy warns.

Heeding her former classmate's words, she looks through her log. There is Travis's name several times but the call never connected.

Talking to Kandy again, she says, "No, only your nosy ass, bitch. You're the only one that held on and listened like some type of pervert."

There is more girly giggling on both ends of the line.

Despite the sour note the day started on, Starr is very happy now.

CHAPTER TWENTY-ONE

Mary is at work but her mind is still playing tricks on her. Maureen, a close friend and coworker, finds Mary in the break room, brooding over her thoughts about her daughter and her lover.

"What is the matter?" Maureen asks as she grabs a cup of coffee. The break room, as it is generously call is a only big enough for a small table with three seats and a counter where the coffee maker and a few dishes are held.

Maureen seats down across from Mary and of course, Mary spills her business, needing someone to unload on.

When she is done telling Maureen about that morning and walking in on Pierre telling Starr she needs to shape up, Maureen says, "That's good and all, that he is telling Starr to respect you guys but it is not appropriate for your man to be in your eighteen year old daughter's bedroom with the door closed."

Mary just cannot contend with the idea that anything is going on between Starr and Pierre and plays devil's advocate.

"I have been knowing this man for five years," she stresses. "He has been in Starr's life for almost as long. Nothing inappropriate is going on. It can't be."

She has left out the fact that Pierre is married to Maureen. She does not need the woman to know that much about their relationship.

Besides, Maureen is of the opinion that all men are dogs and will rut anything if given the chance. Having caught three boyfriends in the act of cheating on her, Maureen is bitter and does not trust the gender. Knowing that Pierre is cheating on his wife with Mary will only reinforce her opinion.

Maureen sips her coffee then replies. "As I said, it's good that he is telling her to respect you but it's not a good idea for them to speak behind closed doors. They could have spoken about whatever they did in front of you."

Mary still excuses the incident and reinforces how Starr had stormed off and Pierre had followed her. They had not intentionally been together alone.

When she is done, Maureen lifts an eyebrow and says, "Okay, Mary but you're playing with fire. Your daughter's hormones are raging and she is technically an adult. And Pierre, well he is a man so…"

Maureen trails off and does not need to say anymore.

Mary hangs her head, the weight on her shoulders even more now. She realizes she hoped secretly that Maureen would reassure that nothing is going on between Pierre and Starr. "You're right," she says softly. "I'll keep a closer eye on Starr. I trust her though. She would never betray me like that even if Pierre did make a move on her."

Mary goes to continue her shift with a heavy heart.

Her bad mood dissipates when she checks her phone later and sees that she received a text from Starr.

I'm sorry for the way I have been acting. Let's have a late lunch when you get off work? My treat.

She smiles to herself. Things are looking up for their mother/daughter relationship.

—⊶⊷—

Mary and Starr are sitting at the restaurant.

The place is rather fancy and Starr had told Mary not to worry about the high prices on the menu when choosing.

Still, when Starr pulls out a rather large sum of cash to pay, Mary has to ask, "Starr, where did you get all that money?"

"Look, Mom, I'm trying to show you a nice time. We have not done much together since graduation," is Starr's answer. Starr is not employed this summer, taking the time to relax before going off to college. There is no way for her to get that kind of money unless...

Then it occurs to Mary.

"Are you seeing someone?" she asks, leaning in closer so that can catch every expression that crosses Starr's face.

A smug look makes the girl's cheeks brighter and she admits, "Yes, I am."

Oh.

That explains so much. A boy can make a girl act crazy!

She smiles and says to her daughter, "That explains it. You're in love."

"Yes, ma'am. I sure am. I sure am."

Mary does not know what to make of the look on Starr's face when she says this. It looks sort of sinister but she must be mistaken.

The waitress interrupts before Mary can ask anymore and the two finish their meal peacefully, such a contrast to the tenseness that existed before Starr's confession.

Before they leave the establishment, there is one thing Mary needs to say.

"Starr, I'm not trying to get in your business. You said you're seeing someone and I'm just trying to look after your happiness.

I don't want you to end up like me, dating a married man. I guess what I am getting at is, please look after yourself and make sure this guy is right for you if you are serious about him."

"Oh, don't worry," Starr waves of Mary's concern. "If I fell for a married man, I would end his marriage."

Mary is horrified at those words and the callous way they are delivered and tries again.

"Well, honey I want whoever you're interested in to be equally interested in you. No one has called the house for you," she tells Starr.

Starr is beginning to get annoyed she can tell and her daughter replies, "My situation is fine, *Mary*. You need to worry about your own relationship. I'm over this meal. I'm ready to go." Starr gets up and walks away, leaving Mary sitting at the table confused and hurt. Starr had never called her by her first name before.

⸺❈⸺

Starr and her mother part ways and Starr heads for the gun store she had visited before.

She got word today that she is approved to purchase the gun and cannot wait pick it up.

She makes her way home afterward.

Luckily, Mary is occupied and she goes into her room to hide the weapon under bed.

After, she lies on her mattress and sighs happily. Step one of her plan is complete.

Her peace and quiet is interrupted by the shrill ring of her phone. She sees Kandy's number and answers.

"The girls and I are going over to the university to a party. You wanna come with us?" Kandy says.

"To the college?" Starr asks, knowing they only go over there she can troll for hot guys. "Oh no, girl. I have a real man to see tonight."

Pierre had texted her that he had something important to tell her earlier and wants to meet up after Mary goes to meet up with an old friend to catch up that afternoon.

Kandy sucks her teeth and says, "Come on, Starr. You can't be serious about your mom's boyfriend?

"What do you mean, Kandy?" Starr asks, starting to get upset. "He is going to be all mine soon. We are going to buy a home, have a family, everything."

"Starr, you really think that man is going to do all that with you? He is *cheating* on your mom with you. Besides, you're going on to college in less than two months. How are you going to buy a house and start a family soon while doing that?" Kandy responds.

Starr has no plans to go to college anymore but she does not tell Kandy that. Instead, she replies, "Are you jealous, bitch? Because you sound a bit green."

The gloves come off then because Kandy comes back with, "You need to check yourself, bitch, because the new you is not it. It was all okay and fine when you guys fucked the first time. A simple fantasy that is it, but now you're acting as if your world revolves around that man."

Starr laughs and replies, "Oh, I get it. You guys, and I know those other two jealous bitches Yvette and Alyssa are there with you, are not happy for me. Well, don't bother calling me again. I'm done with the three of you."

She hangs up before the other girl can say anything else.

CHAPTER TWENTY-TWO

Pierre picks Starr up as promised after Mary leaves for her outing that afternoon.

They drive for a while and he packs the vehicle off to the side of a deserted road.

There is silence and she senses that whatever he has to tell her will leave her very unhappy.

She is right.

"My wife is pregnant."

Starr immediately flushes with something red hot on the inside. It takes a moment for her to realize that it is anger.

No, not anger. That is too mild a word for what she feels imagining Pierre's wife ripe with his child and him staring down at the other woman adoringly.

She is the one who is supposed to be getting round with his offspring. *She* is the one who is supposed to get all his love and adoration. Not Karen, *Starr*.

She looks straight ahead, eyes on the windshield. The violence of her thoughts need to be concealed until she can control them. Try as she might though, she cannot and she turns to him, her movement slow and controlled but vibrating with barely leashed aggression.

"Make her get an abortion," she tells Pierre. He leans back at her demand, clearly startled. "What?" he cries. "An abortion?"

Starr continues deliberately, "I don't want any more stepchildren. One is more than enough. And certainly not before we get married."

Pierre's eyes go round and he says, "Who says we were having children or getting married? Sweetheart, it is going to be you and I no matter what. Stop worrying your pretty little head about these things. You're going to make yourself crazy."

He puts his hand on her thighs, sliding it up and down as he looks away. His response is not what she wants to hear. "Take me home," she tell him.

He sighs but does not argue.

Soon they are back on the highway and headed back to her house.

What neither of them knows it that someone saw them drive off together and it is not just the peeping neighbor.

<hr>

Travis had just been pulling up to Mary's house for a surprise visit with Starr since she seems to be avoiding him when he saw her get into Pierre's vehicle.

Unfortunately, the two had been too far off and he had quickly lost them even though he tried to follow.

He pulls onto the side of the road and calls Mary, brow furrowed with concern and suspicion.

When Mary answers, he does not bother with greetings and gets straight to the point.

"I just saw your man ride off with our daughter," he tells her, the words coming out harsh with his anger at this shady development.

There is a pause and Mary sucks in a breath before saying, "He is only taking her to the celebratory graduation dinner he promised her."

Travis does not like how Mary immediately defends the man. "And you're sure that's what they are doing?" he asks.

"Well, he has not taken her yet. Where else would they be going?" she answers and before he can say anything else, she adds, "I need to go now. I am meeting up with a friend and she just arrived."

She hangs up.

A burst of frustration has Travis throwing his phone into the passenger seat.

It lands with a thud as he stares off in the direction Starr and Pierre went.

Oh, I am right about that man taking advantage of my daughter and I am going to prove it one way or the other, he thinks.

Mary is seating in a restaurant waiting for her girlfriend. She lied to Travis about the woman arriving already.

She cannot answer his questions because the answers leave her back at square one – doubting the loyalty of two people she should be able to trust.

And she is not ready to face that reality. "Hey, Mary," she hears.

She looks up to find her childhood friend, Carmen rushing toward her with a smile on her face.

She answers with one of her own and gets up to hug the woman. Inside though, her heart is breaking with doubt and a growing, nagging suspicion.

CHAPTER TWENTY-THREE

That night Mary and Starr are having dinner together.

Mary had a hard time getting her daughter to join her. Although Starr was home when she got back home, the girl has been in a terrible mood and snaps at her mother with very little provocation. Mary is trying to be patient but it is very difficult not snapping right back at the teenager.

The two are sitting in the living room. A popular TV show is playing while the two eat their macaroni and cheese dinner.

She looks her daughter over, trying to be subtle. Despite Starr's less than welcoming personality lately, she still cannot concede that this girl would betray her by having a relationship with Pierre behind her back. Starr is her child. There is no way her own flesh and blood, a girl that she created within her own body would do this to her.

Right?

"So," Mary starts. "This new boyfriend of yours. When can I meet him?"

Starr does not look at Mary but Mary sees her body briefly tense before she answers, "You will not like him so there is no point in you two meeting."

Before Mary can responds, Starr gets up and says, "I am going to my room. I have suddenly lost my appetite."

The girl's bedroom door closes soon after, leaving behind a defeated-feeling Mary

Needing answers, she grabs the telephone and calls Pierre.

"Why didn't you tell me that you picked Starr up today?" she asks him after he greets her.

There is a pause and then says, "I took her out for that dinner I told you about."

"Why didn't you tell me you guys were going today?" she insists. "I just did not mention it, alright. It is no big deal. When I used to pick her up from school without your permission you did not trip. Are you trying to insinuate something?"

He sounds defensive and it raises her hackles. But then she realizes that she has nothing solid to base her suspicions on and she feels foolish.

That defeated feeling comes at her again and she slumps where she sits, looking at the ceiling as if it has the answers to her questions.

In her subdue voice, she says, "I'm sorry, baby. I didn't mean to insinuate anything. I'm just going through some things and I guess, I took it out on you."

She sighs when he hangs up without accepting her apology. Listlessness now, she goes to Starr's room and knocks on the door.

No answer.

"Starr? Baby, are you awake?" she calls and still no answer. She turns the lock and goes in.

She finds Starr sitting at her makeup table still fully clothed. Starr is just staring at the mirror, a glazed look in her eyes.

"Why didn't you answer me?" she asks her daughter but instead of getting an answer, Starr snaps, "Why are you invading my privacy? Is that what you do when I am not here? Just barge in?" Taken aback and already reeling from her conversation with Pierre, Mary automatically tries to diffuse the situation and says, "No, honey, I just wanted to make sure that you are okay."

Starr gets up and advances on Mary. There is a crazed look in her eyes that has Mary backing away like an animal that is being threatened. Before she knows, she is back over the threshold of Starr's bedroom.

"Don't just bust in my room like that ever again."

With those word, Starr slams the door in her mother's face.

CHAPTER TWENTY-FOUR

Morning has comes and Pierre has spent the whole day with his wife.

He offered to take her shopping and she agreed after he told her he wanted them to spend more time together to solve the problems in their relationship. She had lit up when he said that. They are his SUV and getting on the freeway. Pierre speeds up and Karen moves to put on her seatbelt.

Suddenly he mashes the brakes and she goes slamming into the dash, knocked unconscious immediately. A cut on her head begins to bleed profusely.

He takes his seatbelt off and shakes her, shouting, "Honey, honey! Karen, talk to me. Are you okay?"

She does not respond and he grabs his cell phone to call 911. He gives his location and waits until they arrive, ignoring the honking and hollering of the traffic around him.

Although it seems like forever, soon Karen is loaded up into an ambulance.

He follows closely behind the vehicle with blazing sirens and paces the halls of the hospital for hours as he awaits news on Karen's condition.

She was taken into the emergency room and he was barred from entering.

When the doctors comes out to talk to him, he hears nothing else the man has to say except, "I am sorry, sir, but your wife has miscarried."

He is allowed to see Karen who has been placed in a private room. She is asleep and a white bandage has been taped across her head. She looks very pale and fragile.

He cannot bear to look at her for long and leaves the hospital in a near run. He gets in his vehicle and drives off.

He stops a few miles away and rests his hands on the steering wheel. He puts his head down too, really shaken up by the whole ordeal.

Then he smiles, still on the adrenaline high.

He grabs his cell phone suddenly and calls Starr.

She picks up on the third ring and before she can say anything, he goes, "I did it, Starr! I did it!"

"What?" she asks and she sounds rather formal, probably still ticked off at him, he guesses.

"Karen lost the baby," he tells her.

Still not catching his drift, she asks, "She aborted it?"

"No, she didn't abort it. I caused an accident and she's at the hospital now," he announces, feeling proud of himself.

He had been horrified when Starr had suggested the idea of getting rid of the unborn child but after marinating on it, the idea grew on him quickly. He does not want a baby to care for right now or ever again.

He knows that Karen will never willingly abort a child so he took matters into his own hands and it worked out marvelously.

Starr laughs and praises, "Oh, I like your style baby." All stiffness is gone from her voice now.

"Can I see you?" she asks in a purring tone that has him imagining all sorts of tantalizing and illicit things.

"Yeah, let me arrange things. I'll call you later," he tells her.

He gets back on the road shortly after, feeling light and happy.

CHAPTER TWENTY-FIVE

In the following days, Pierre hangs around Mary's house a lot more than usual.

With Karen in the hospital, he has lots of free time now. He has stopped by to see her twice in the four day period, both times to drop off supplies that she needs for her stay.

He kept the visits very short and hardly looked her in the eye when he was there.

He ignores most of her calls to his cell phone.

Mary has come down with a bug in that time and has been taking some medication to help ease the symptoms. The medication is leaving her feeling super drowsy and she sleeps a lot, which gives him and Starr plenty of time to hang out and be intimate.

Mary told him that it renews her feelings for Pierre that he has been around and helping her out in this difficult time for her. He is glad for her feelings because it pushes aside the suspicions she was beginning to have about him and Starr.

Best of all, Starr has been in good spirits most of the time, not busting his chops or snapping at her mother so often.

Things have been very calm and peaceful. Tonight he is picking up both Starr and Mary and taking them to dinner.

He knocks on the door and Mary shouts, "Pierre, is that you?" "Yeah."

"Come in. The door is open," she says.

So he lets himself in. The kitchen and living room are empty. "Are you ladies ready?" he asks.

"Just a minute," Mary's voice comes from the direction of her bedroom.

He makes himself comfortable on the couch. He leans back only to sit up straight again when Starr comes into the space.

She is all done up in a figure-hugging dresses and high heels, and looks absolutely gorgeous. It reminds him of how she looked on her prom night and the possessive feelings that had run through him then return with a vengeance.

He gulps then tells her, "Oh my god, baby. You look extraordinary."

Their moment is interrupted by Mary yelling, "A few more minutes, Pierre. Starr will be done soon, too."

Clearly, she does not know that Starr has already joined Pierre in the living room.

"Okay," he yells back and stands.

Going up to Starr, he puts his hands around her waist and whispers in her ear, "I want to take you right here and now. I'm at the point where I'll risk it all. I don't care."

He knows that he is saying exactly what she wants to hear. She brightens up at this words and strokes her hands up his arms.

"I don't care either," she tells him. "We can get rid of her and be together."

He has to slow things down now and says, "Whoa, whoa, baby. Wait a minutes. Let's not rush things."

This is not a talk he wants to have now so he distracts her by putting a hand on her breast. He kisses her cleavage and licks all the way up to her neck.

Right before his lips touch hers, they hear footsteps coming down the hall and spring apart.

When Mary enters the living room, he says, "Oh, Mary, you look great."

Mary lights up and indicates Starr, saying, "You see where she gets her beauty from then."

She is teasing and laughs her own joke.

Pierre goes, "No doubt. You women are very beautiful. You certainly get it from your mom, Starr."

Starr rolls her eyes and makes an uncommitted sound.

They head out shortly after. Pierre takes them to an upscale Italian restaurant.

They get seated with Mary and Pierre on one side while Starr is on the other of the table.

While the waitress is taking their orders, Pierre cannot resist and plays footsies with Starr under the table.

This continues as the food arrives and they eat. Everyone seems to be enjoying themselves and it is the way Pierre wants it.

The mood gets interrupted when Mary's phone keeps on vibrating from inside her purse.

Eventually, he asks, "Are you going to get that?"

She pulls out the device and he gets a look at the screen. Travis's name shows up on the caller ID.

Pierre gets irritated.

She is on a date with me and entertaining her ex?

Talk about gull!

"Why does he keep on calling you like that? What can he possibly want to say to you at this hour of the night?" he demands

"Um," she says, looking away. "I don't know what he wants but I am sure it can wait until later. I won't answer it."

She cancels the call and turns her phone off quickly. She picks up the glass of wine she has been sipping all night and finishes the rest in one gulp.

She gestures at the waitress for more.

Starr turns to her mother with a smirk and comments, "Why won't you answer it, Mom. You always talk to dad late at night." Mary looks at Mary. "What do you mean, I always talk to your dad?"

"Oh, you guys are always on the phone and he is always around, especially since that night he slept over."

Starr looks so innocent and clueless as she says this but Pierre knows what she is doing.

Mary laughs and the sound comes out nervously.

"Oh, well. We just talk about how he wants to get back on track with his life and reconnect with you," she explains, the words rushing out.

Starr goes, "Hmmm-mmm, Mom. You know Dad still likes you." "It doesn't really matter if he does," Mary stammers. "I'm with Pierre and that is who I want to be with."

Although entertained by Mary's discomfort, Pierre says, "Enough, enough. Let's not ruin the evening talking about him. He's a loser."

Starr instantly agrees, "Right."

Mary's eyes jump between Pierre and Starr. "Don't talk about Travis like that. He deserves respect as Starr's father."

Starr rolls her eyes and says, "Let's just change the subject." Pierre gets up and says, "I need to go wash my hands."

He walks away.

—⦿⦿⦿—

When Pierre is out of earshot, Mary leans over the table, closer to Starr and hisses, "Why the hell would you say these things?" Sarcasm dripping from her voice, Starr replies, "You always tell me to be honest. You always tell me to never play with a good man's heart. Dad left us with no regard to how either of us felt.

He just shows up again and all of a sudden he is spending the night. That's not right, Mom. That is so disrespectful to Pierre and to me."

Mary leans back and looks away, clearly feeling ashamed. "You're right. That was bad judgment on my part. I'm only human though, Starr. I make mistakes. But Pierre does not now that Travis and I slept toge-"

Mary catches herself and stops, her eyes jumping guiltily to Starr's. She starts drinking more wine and before Starr's eyes drains yet another glass. The waitress had left the bottle and she pours herself more.

"What?" Starr shrieks. "Slept together?"

I knew it, she thinks.

Mary does not bother lying and tells Starr, "Yes, we slept together and Pierre does not know that. It was a one time thing. I was upset and lonely. You don't understand what it feel like to be a single mom and have no one to turn to. Sometimes you need affection. You're a young lady now. You know that."

"Hmmm-mmm," Starr goes, shaking her head in clear disgust. "I need to wash my hands too."

Mary is drinking more wine as she get up from the table and head to the restroom area. Instead of going to the women's facilities, she goes to the men's.

Pierre is leaning against the wall inside and smiles when he sees her.

"I knew that you would come," he tells her.

She rushes to him and embraces him. Between kisses, she outs her mom by saying, "You have my mom all kinds of tied up. She just confessed to fucking my dad to me."

He laughs. "Watch how I fuck her daughter."

He pulls up her dress and soon has her pinned against the wall and penetrated.

While he sexes her rough, she keeps on repeating, "I love you." "I know you do," he tells her.

Their loving is quick but leaves them both very satisfied.

⸺⸽⸻

Starr and Pierre have been gone for a long time, Mary thinks hazily.

She takes another gulp of wine.

She knows that she should not be drinking so heavily, especially since she is taking medication but she needs the pain soothing effects.

She gets up on shaky legs and goes to look for Starr and Pierre. She goes into the women's restroom and finds Starr washing her hands. Her hair is stilled mused and Mary wonders what could have caused that. Looking harder, Mary sees that Starr's dressed is a little wrinkled too.

"What happened?" she asks and hears the slur in her words. "Oh!" Starr looks up, startled to see her. "I threw up a little and I am just tidying up."

"Oh no, honey. Are you alright? I came to search for you because I was worried. You were gone for so long."

She helps Starr compose herself as best she can in her inebriated state and the two leave the restroom together.

Pierre is already back at the table when they get there.

They do not stay long after that and soon Pierre is helping Mary to the SUV. The whole bottle of wine had been emptied before they left.

———⌘———

Starr giggles softly behind Mary's back as Pierre helps her mother get across the parking lot.

Mary is tripping over her own two feet, swaying left and right and acting the fool, giggling one moment then seeming on the verge of tears the next.

"Oh my god. I'm so embarrassed. I should not have drank that much," Mary says, hiccupping around her words and clinging to Pierre for balance.

Starr fights another giggle at behavior she sees as childish. She feels like the adult instead of her mother.

She goes close to Pierre's other side and he intertwines their fingers.

She squeezes his hands, feeling on top of the world right now.

The relationship between Pierre and Mary is falling apart. Maybe she does not have to use that gun to get Mary out of the picture after all.

Pierre drives them back to the house. Mary falls asleep not even five minutes into the ride and Pierre has to carry her in when they reach their destination.

She is half awake when he enter her bedroom and groans.

"It's okay, babe. I've got you," he tells her but his attention is over his shoulder because Starr has lifted her dress and pushed her panties down her legs. She makes suggestive motions at him and he is instantly ready for her. She winks at him and goes in the direction of her bedroom.

She gets out of her clothes, puts on a tiny pair of pajamas then goes back in search of Pierre. He has already put Mary in her bed, taken off her shoes and tucked her in. Her eyes are closed again and her breathing is steady.

Still, Starr brings her mother two extra strength muscle relaxers and helps Mary take them.

Only a few minutes later, Starr picks up her mother's arm and it drops back in position heavily. Starr repeats this and the same thing happens. Mary is out cold.

She and Pierre smile at each other and leave Mary's bedroom, locking it behind them.

Starr leads Pierre to a side of the living room where they can hear if Mary happens to get up.

Pierre sits on the couch and Starr gets on her knees between his legs and pleasures him that way for the first time.

Headlights flash through the windows facing the driveway but the two do not stop what they are doing.

When Mary had not picked up his call, Travis got worried and is driving by her house now but as he pulls up he sees Pierre's SUV parked right next to her car.

He wants to go in there and force the man out of the house and away from Mary and Starr. His hand is on the door and his body is tight with need to do just that but he stops himself.

For the first time, he doubts that he can reclaim his family like he wants.

So, he pulls back out of the driveway and drives off.

After giving Pierre the release he needs. Starr goes into the bathroom to wash out her mouth.

She goes back into the living room but he is nowhere to be found. He is gone.

When she checks her cell phone, she sees a message from him. *I had a great time tonight. See you are the barbeque this weekend. XOXO*

CHAPTER TWENTY-SIX

Travis and Starr are driving back to her house from the mall. It is the weekend of Starr going away celebration. She had completely forgotten about the event to recognize her going to college soon. All the neighbors and their family had been invited to the huge cook up in Mary's backyard.

It is a wasted celebration because she is not going anywhere and leaving her man behind.

As part of the celebration, Travis had taken Starr out shopping and told her to pick out whatever she wanted. There were a few bags in the backseat with all the stuff she back chosen.

Travis has been playing the part of devoted father, stopping by a lot lately and trying to spend time with her.

She doesn't know how she feels about it. Sometimes, it feels good to have her dad back and other times, she just wants him to go away.

He is not the one on her mind right now though.

He is speaking to her yet she does not hear a word he says because she is daydreaming about Pierre.

She is looking out the window and the sights of the city pass her unseen.

Travis tries to pull Starr out of her daze with a few questions and she gives him the shortest answers possible.

When they get back to the house, she jumps out immediately.

There are already a lot of guests there and music is playing. There is the smell of the barbeque perfuming the air.

She follows the action to the backyard. She had not spotted Pierre's vehicle when she and Travis pulled up but she sees him at the grill with Mary.

She becomes tunnel visioned. She wants to make a beeline to him and throw herself into his arms.

She feels a huge smile light her face as she looks at him. He looks back at her as if sensing her gaze and she cannot deny the urge. She starts moving toward him and passes a neighbor living directly across the street. The woman gives her a weird look that she pays no attention to.

She ignores it when the woman leans over to whisper something to another woman who lives a few house down the street.

She had forgotten that Mary is standing next to Pierre so focused on him but Mary turns when Starr is only inches away from the man she intended to embrace like he belongs to her.

"Hey, baby," Mary greets, jolting Starr out of her daze. "How do you like the party? It is all about you today."

Hearing Mary's voice causes something to break inside Starr. She is tired of sharing Pierre. Tired of hiding her love and desire for him. It is not fair, dammit!

She feels her face crumble and the tears are coming.

She turns around and runs to the house. She pushes people out of her way and the confused looks on their faces make it harder to hold her composure.

———◦∞◦———

The vibe at the party is very awkward after Starr disappears into the house, clearly distressed. Whispers start up and fingers point. Mary looks in the direction that her daughter went in confusion before turning back to Pierre.

"What just happened?" she asks.

"I have no clue," Pierre answers and quickly turns back to man the grill.

She sees Travis heading to the house, after Starr. She heads after him.

Starr is stopped before she reaches her bedroom by her father. He grabs her arms and turns around to face him.

"What's going on with you, Starr?" he asks.

She ducks her head to hide her expression when she answers, "It's nothing. I just started cramping suddenly. I just need to rest and be alone for a little while."

She hopes he takes the hint and leaves her be. "Oh, okay," he says and leaves to go outside.

Mary does not understand why people are getting up to leave but she has to tend to her daughter now and does not concern herself with it.

She is already halfway to the house when she hears a neighbor says, "You know, the Johnsons saw him leaving with her daughter and they were really cozy if you know what I mean."

Mary turns around and spins the woman who had uttered the words around. Renee is her name and she is a known gossip in the community.

The middle-aged African-American woman is startled and her eyes widen.

"What did you say?" Mary demands.

Stammering, the woman quickly answers, "N-nothing."

She shakes off Mary's grips and puts her drinks down before taking off faster than Mary has ever seen her move before.

She leaves the party and those who do not follow up turn their eyes away from Mary, leaving her feeling like everyone knows something she does not. She even noticed a few pointed fingers moving between her, Pierre and the direction Starr went.

That feeling in her chest that she has been trying to ignore grows.

<hr />

Starr is on her bed and holding the gun she purchased.

She is rocking back and forth, her mind going a thousand miles per second.

If it was not for that bitch, he would be mine, she thinks.

Her mother's smiling face flashes in her bed and seems to mock her.

What if the bitch never unleashes her claws from Pierre, she wonders.

It physically hurts to think about and all she wants is for it to stop. She cannot fathom not having him all to herself soon. She puts the gun to her head.

If she cannot live in this world with the man she loves then she would rather not live at all.

The gun is unsteady against her skin from her shaking hands. She stands and begins to pace, the gun still against her head. "Someone will die," she whispers to herself over and over again. "If I can't be with him, no one will."

Suddenly there is a knocks at the door. "Starr?" comes Mary's voice.

She is startled and drops the gun on the floor. It lands with a loud thud.

"Leave me alone," she screams.

Mary hangs her head against Starr's locked bedroom door. She is fighting tears, so many emotion making it difficult to think.

Why can't I get through to my daughter, she wonders to herself. Pierre comes up behind Mary and says, "Just leave her be, Mary."

He grabs her gently by the shoulder and brings her to her bedroom.

When he lets her go, she looks him in the eye and says, "Is there something between you and Starr that I need to know?"

Anger flashes in his eyes and his hands go to his hips.

He paces away then turns back to her and hisses, "What the hell do you mean? What the hell are you talking about?"

She is getting angry too and motions heatedly as she tells him, "I have never had a strained relationship with my daughter until recently. You've been pulling back from me too lately. Is that just a coincident, Pierre? And it is not just I who has noticed these changes. Her father has seen it too."

"And you seem to be forgetting that *he* has just recently popped up out of nowhere too? Maybe you should be thinking that Starr is confused and needs a consistent male figure in her life instead of trying to blame me," he says, his voice getting louder. "Of course, I have been close to her. I am the only father figure she has known for the longest time. She is like my own daughter and you're going to stand there and accuse me off some bullshit while giving that deadbeat of a dad credit. How dare you? You need to shape up

Mary and stopping letting that guy influence your thinking. He has already left you and Starr for dead and you are stupidly letting him into your lives again so that history can repeat itself."

Mary is flabbergasted by his outburst and gets an attitude. "Excuse you," she reproaches.

"No," he interrupts her. "You're the one who needs to be excused, coming at me sideways like that. I resent the things you are insinuating and I have to think long and hard before I can forgive you."

He walks out with the last word.

She hears his vehicle door slam and her feet move without her consent. She follows him and standing in the front door, she sees him slamming his hands against the steering wheel.

He picks up his cell phone and puts it against his ear. Suddenly she can hear Starr's phone ringing.

It stop and she sees Pierre's lips moving through the closed glass. It clicks in her head.

This sonofabitch is talking to my daughter, she thinks.

She runs to Starr's bedroom and, banging on the closed door, she yells, "Starr! Starr, who are you talking to?"

There is talking from the other side then silence.

Mary bangs the wood some more than suddenly falls forward as the door is opened.

Starr stands before her, looking calm and composed. She pushed Starr back inside and Starr falls to the floor.

"Are you talking to who I think you're talking to?" Mary shouts. Starr looks at her confused. Picking herself up, Starr asks Mary, "Are you crazy?"

Mary spies Starr's phone on the floor. She grabs it and with a few swipes of her fingers goes down the call log.

She does not see Pierre's number at all.

The wind in her sail go out and she is left breathing heavily and wondering if she is going crazy.

She feels those tears coming again and starts to apologize to her daughter but Starr gets in her face and points at the door, saying, "Get out of my room."

Mary starts, "But-" Starr screams, "Now!"

"But I thought- I thought... Never mind what I thought," she says.

She hands Start her phone back and walks away. Starr slams the bedroom door behind her.

I should have never listened to Travis, she thinks.

Starr leans against the close door.

Phew, a good thing she had time delete Pierre's call log before Mary barged in here.

CHAPTER TWENTY-SEVEN

Travis is getting the cold shoulder from both Mary and Starr.

He has tried to call and visit in the last two days since the failed barbeque but the roadblocks are popping up everywhere.

Since he cannot get through to either of his girls, he decides to focus on finding out what is going on between Pierre and Starr.

All he wants to do is get his family back but using the direct approach has not worked so far. So it is time to try something different.

He has decided to pay Pierre a visit.

He found out where the man works and is waiting to catch sight of him in the parking lot. He is in luck because he spies Pierre coming out of the building not long after he pulls up.

Pierre is on the phone when he notices Travis leaning against his vehicle.

He looks startled then he says something to the person on the line and hangs up.

He goes up to Travis and very cockily asks, "To what do I owe the pleasure of this impromptu meeting?"

Travis does not have time to play these games so he gets right to the point. "What's going on between you and my daughter?"

Pierre scoffs and tells him, "Move away from my vehicle or I will be forced to call the police."

Arrogance oozes off this man and rubs Travis the wrong way. Still, he does as Pierre says because he cannot afford to go back to jail.

He watches the other man get in the car and roll the window down.

"You should not worry about things so much, dude. I am taking care of *both* Mary and Starr real good," he tells Travis, smirking.

Travis steps closer to the vehicle. "And what the fuck does that mean?"

"You're not the brightest crayon in the box but I am sure even you can figure it out."

With these parting words, Pierre rolls up the windows and drives away before Travis can do anything.

Travis is left with a burning rage.

Pierre drove to his house after the confrontation with Travis.

He feels good having had the last word and knocking the other man down a peg or two.

Who does Travis think he is coming at him like that anyway?

He shakes his head at the man's audacity. He puts Travis out of his mind when he pulls into his driveway.

He took the rest of the day off work to spend with Karen. She is back at home now but is pissed at him for not being at the hospital more and ignoring her phone calls. She had had to take a cab home since he had not known when her release day was. She has even mentioned thinking about getting a divorce.

He cannot have that so he is putting in the work to get back into her good graces.

Plus, he kind of feels bad about causing the accident.

He looks at his phone before he goes in. There are four missed calls from Starr. He has not seen her since the fiasco of a barbeque and has not talked to her on the phone either. She needs to learn to control herself feelings more or she will get them both caught. He is teaching her a lesson by ignoring her attempts at communication.

He makes sure the phone is on silent and puts it away.

When he gets inside, he announces his presence and tries to hug his wife when he finds her in the kitchen.

First she tries to pull away but he persist, apologizing and complimenting her, and she melts into his body.

That marks the beginning of the day wooing his wife. She is wary but does not stop his attempt.

It is late evening when he is startled to see Starr standing in his front yard. It is very dark but still, he makes her out. She is looking into the window and her eyes are trained on where his hands are around Karen's waist. There is rage in her eyes when they lift to his.

He almost curses out loud but manages to control himself.

Trying to control the situation, he leans over to whisper in Karen ear and convinces her that they should go upstairs to get ready for bed.

He looks out onto the front lawn again when they get there but there is no sign of Starr.

He and 'Karen get into bed about an hour later. She falls asleep almost immediately but he is too tense to.

His eyes are closed when he suddenly feels someone staring at him.

When he opens them Starr is standing there right next to his marital bed. He begins sweating.

Bewildered, nervous and a little frightened, he does not move as he watches her watching him as she strips out of her clothes. She has a sinister smile on her face and a far-off look in her eyes.

He wants to tell her to stop what she is doing but does not want to risk waking his wife.

His mind is going in circles.

How did she get in?

Why is she here?

Why is she stripping?

He is afraid of what she will do next but she only picks up her clothes off from where she dropped them on the floor and leaves the room quietly.

Untangling himself from Karen's hold, he goes after Starr quietly, rushing downstairs.

He only finds the front door open with no sign of Starr.

He shuts it and stands there in disbelief.

He turns to go back upstairs and is frightened anew when he sees Karen standing at the top.

"Where are you coming from?" she asks.

"I thought I heard something outside but it was nothing, baby," he explains.

She leads him back to bedroom and while she sleeps, he is left shaken and unable to.

Starr drives around for awhile after she leaves Pierre's house but finally stops at a bar.

Her dashboard lets her know it is after midnight but she has no fear for her safety.

She is here on a mission and she just has to find a willing participant to accomplish what she wants.

She finds him immediately upon entering the bar.

She meets the attractive man's eyes and that easily, she has him hooked.

He approaches her and offers to buy her a drink.

Starr hardly ever drinks but still accepts his offer because she is mad at her man.

"I am pissed at my man," she tells him as they sip on their beers. "Do you want to help piss him off with me?"

"Anything to help a sexy little thing like you," he replies.

She is going to teach Pierre a lesson by sleeping with this stranger.

"Then let's get out of here," she says.

They do not finish their drinks and he leads her to his car.

While he drives, he reaches over and fondles her thighs and breasts. She does not know where he is going and does not care.

She is not turned on by his clumsy attempts but does not stop him.

He stops the car soon and it is next to a beautiful lake. The moonlight makes the surface shimmer as if there are diamonds.

They both get out of the car. He pulls a blanket out of the back and lays it on the ground near the edge of the water. They get on it.

He is kissing on her and trying to get her clothes off when she asks, "Do you have a girlfriend?"

"Yes," he says, no shame.

Starr gets mad and pushes at his shoulders.

"Why are you here with me then?" she asks.

His reply is, "Shut up and come take this dick."

He is bigger than her and stronger so Starr pretends submission, saying, "Okay."

As he leans back toward her, she shifts and pushes him with all her might.

He falls back and splashes into the lake.

"You should not cheat on your woman," Starr yells at the philandering man.

She turns around and runs to his car, fleeing the scene. She does not turn back and collects her car for the bar, unaware and uncaring if he is dead or alive.

She gets back home after four in the morning.

She gets into bed and falls asleep just as she is, makeup and all.

The next morning, she wakes up with a plan and a look of determination.

CHAPTER TWENTY-EIGHT

Karen is sitting at home.

She is on a sofa placed near a window, facing the front of the house.

Her mind is far off as she allows her body to heal from its ordeal. Namely, it is on her husband and what she should do about their relationship.

Karen loves her husband but wonders if constantly dealing with the idea that he is unfaithful is worth staying in this marriage.

The telephone rings, jolting her out of her depressive reverie.

She gets up slowly to pick up the line and answers, "Hello?"

"I did it, Starr! I did it!" she hears Pierre say.

She opens her mouth to ask what but another female voice comes across the telephone and asks the questions before she does, "What?"

"Karen lost the baby," Pierre tells the other female and Karen realizes that she is listening to a recording by the echo she hears as she listens.

"She aborted it?" the unknown female says and Karen's fingers tighten on the phone. They are talking about her and her lost baby and for that alone, Karen feels betrayed. She does not know this woman yet Pierre is confiding personal information about their relationship with her.

"No, she didn't abort it. I caused an accident and she's at the hospital now," Pierre's voice announces, sounding very proud.

Karen is horrified and tears fill her eyes immediately. She cannot believe what she just heard.

I must be dreaming, she rationalizes to herself but her brain tells her different. She is very much awake.

There is a click then the recording is replaced by the same female voice.

"Hello, bitch. I bet you're speechless from what you just heard so I'll do the talking. Pierre is my man now. We're going to get married and make lots of beautiful babies of our own. Just to prove it to you, I will be sending you a whole lot more recordings of our conversations. Don't try to hold onto him because he is mine now and I am fed up of sharing."

The line goes dead.

Karen takes the phone away from her ear and stares at it in shocked disbelief. She pinches herself to make sure that she is indeed awake because she just cannot believe her life has turned to this.

Then her cell phone begins beeping from nearby with incoming messages. She drops the phone that she is holding and it smashes to pieces at her feet.

Like a zombie, she walks over to her cell phone and picks it up and opens the recording contained within the first message.

When she is done with that one she opens another and another. They range from Pierre dirty talking to the obviously very young woman to arranging to pick her up on days that he excused his absence from his and Karen's marital bed on work.

Then she gets to the last, the one of him admitting to him causing her to lose their baby on the highway that fateful morning.

The sun is high in the air by the time she is done listening.

She is devastated and so very hurt.

She married this man.

She loves him

She thought he loved her too.

She has never been so wrong in her life.

He is selfish and cruel and does not love anyone else but himself.

Her fingers dial his number without much command from her brain.

He does not answer and she keeps on redialing over and over again.

She does not really know why she needs to talk to him now when she knows she will not be able to stand the sound of his voice. Maybe for him to tell her it really is not true. That this is some kind of sick joke.

She breaks down then, falling to her knees and crying over all the wasted years of her life. She cries because she ignored the signs of his cheating and often excused his behavior. She has known it for years - something in her soul telling her so – and all this time he really has been stepping out on her.

And finally, she cries for her unborn baby, a child who was not given a chance at life because his father is a self-entitled psychopath.

Finally, she wipes her cheeks and makes up her mind.

She dials 911. She tells them that he caused the loss of her baby and she has the tape to prove it.

She hangs up with the promise that detectives would be at her house in a few minutes.

The police department holds true to its promise and two uniformed men knock on her door less than half an hour later. The Caucasian men show her their badges and she invites them in.

She tells him everything and gives them the recording this "Starr" has sent to her.

"We will get him for this, ma'am," one says and that is exactly what she wants.

———— ❧ ————

Pierre sees his cells phone light up from the dashboard of his vehicle yet again.

It is Starr.

She has been calling him nonstop and so has Karen.

He ignores both their calls. He has a lot on his mind and does not want to deal with either of them right now.

Starr's behavior is getting out of hand and he needs to figure out how to handle her. He cannot just break it off with her. As the night before proves, she is unstable and who knows what she will do if he goes that route.

Besides, he is not ready to give up sexing her yet. She is by far the most addictive person in the sack.

He drives around for a long time and gets no closer to a solution so he heads home midafternoon.

He turns the corner into his street and presses on the brakes.

There is a police car parked in his driveway.

His heart immediately starts to pound in his chest.

He tells himself he is panicking for no reason. Karen could not have found out about what he did. No one knows except Starr-

Shit!

He throws his vehicle in reverse and speeds away.

When he thinks he is far enough away, he stops and calls home and pretends he is finally answering Karen's call.

"Hello, honey?" he says when his wife answers. "Did you call me?"

Karen immediately begins screaming.

"I know what you did, you bastard! Your stupid mistress sent me the tape. You're going to pay for this, Pierre. I will make sure of it! I am filling charges. You're going to spend the rest of your miserable life rotting in prison."

That is some shuffle on the line then a man's voice comes on.

"Good day, sir. You are wanted for question in connection-"

Pierre does not listen to the rest. He hangs up and turns off his cell phone.

He sits there for a long time, just looking out the windscreen.

He can see his perfect life falling out of his grasp. His job, his house, car, everything. He will lose it all, all because Starr is being an idiot!

He knows that she is young and impulse, but to give him up like that! What the hell was she thinking?

He is good and mad when he pulls back onto the road. A plan has formed in his head and he races over to Mary's house.

He parks haphazardly in her driveway and runs up to her front door, banging on the door.

Mary answers and looks at him in surprise.

She grabs his arm and pulls him inside.

"Pierre, what's wrong? What's wrong?" she keeps on repeating.

He is sweating and trembling and obviously in distress.

Panting, he says, "I can't live without you, Mary. I'm leaving *her* and I want us to be together. Just the two of us. I know that things have been weird between us and only escalated at the barbeque but I want to put all of that behind us and have a happy future together."

He pulls her into a tight up, noticing the shocked look on her face before she returns his embrace.

When he pulls back, she is smiling.

He retunes a smile he hopes looks equally happy.

She does not need to know that he is only here because his wife had called the cops on him for intentionally aborting their baby and he cannot go home. And that she only found out because Mary's daughter outed him because he is sleeping with her and she is bitter because he was ignoring her.

Yeah, Mary certainty does not need to know those details.

He clears his throat and asks, "She kicked me out when I told her I want to be with you. Can I stay here?"

"Of course, baby. Stay as long as you need," Mary tell him.

That is exactly what he wants to here.

"Did you bring your clothes with you?" she questions.

"Uh no, the falling out between Karen and I was really bad and I did not have a chance to grab anything. And it's probably best I do not go back there until she calms down. That will probably be quite a while since she was so pissed at me."

"Oh, okay, well we'll get you some stuff soon."

"Great!"

"Starr will be thrilled when she finds out you're staying over," Mary says, walking away.

Lucky she did that because Pierre is sure he had not hidden his facial expressions very well at the mention on the traitor. Mary does not seem to hold any grudge over their quarrel at the barbeque and he is not going to do anything to make her upset.

"I bet she will," he answers mildly.

Mary turns back to him and pats his cheek affectionately. He schools him face into a pleasant expression as she says, "I never thought we would be together like this but I am so very happy that you're here. We can start a life together the right way and set a good example for Starr."

"That we can," he agrees. "That we can."

Then he goes on, "I was thinking that I want a clean slate with you, Mary. We can get a new place together, maybe move out of state too. With Starr going off to college soon, there would be nothing tying you down here. We can travel and see the world together. I'd take care of you, of course."

Mary's eyes are wide when she asks, "But what about your job?"

"I can get another job. Maybe even change my name legally. A completely new start. What do you think?"

She searches his eyes. "You're serious about this?"

"Absolutely."

"Oh okay. Well, I'll think about all that you've said."

He needs her to more than think about it. He needs to get out of town soon and does not have time to waste.

But he needs Mary for now so he smiles hugely and says, "That is all I ask babe. As long as you're with me, I'm a happy man."

CHAPTER TWENTY-NINE

Starr has been driving around all day, looking for Pierre.

He was supposed to have called her by now since Karen knows what he did. Karen should have broken things off with him and he should have come running to Starr, begging for them to be together forever.

Pierre is not doing what he is supposed to do and it is making her increasingly angry.

Her fingers tighten on the steering wheel.

She has driven through his neighborhood several times today but has seen no sign of him.

Her mind is far, trying to figure where else she can locate him when she is jolted from her musing by the loud honk of a horn. She swerves to avoid hitting an oncoming vehicle and ends up on the side of the road. She had driving into opposing traffic and had not realized.

She is trembling and panicked but luckily safe.

She puts her head on the wheel and tries to pull herself together.

She is tired and hungry, having not eaten in over twenty-four hours. She had gotten out of bed early this morning and left in the same clothes she wore yesterday. Luckily, Mary had already left the house by the time she had gotten up so she had had no explanations to make as she dashed out.

Her only thought had been implementing her new plans. Then all her dreams would come true, she had thought.

So far nothing is working out as planned though and she is wary.

She pulls back onto the highway, heading home.

She needs to rest and eat and then she will be able to figure out want to do about her situation. About how to make Pierre all hers and hers alone.

It is late evening when she pulls up in front of her mother's house. To her surprise, Pierre's truck is parked in the driveway.

A host of emotion flood her as she sees this and she fights to calm her nerves.

She knows that he will likely be mad at what she did but he will see that it is for the best so that they can be together soon enough.

She looks in the rearview mirror, checking her makeup. She fixes her hair and adjusts her outfit, wanting to look perfect for Pierre.

She takes a deep breath and gets out of the car.

She enters the home and tries to act like everything is normal.

"Hello, everybody. What's up?" she shouts out.

She enters the kitchen and finds Pierre and Mary there. Pierre is sitting at the table while Mary is busy at the stove. By the smell of it, Mary has started on dinner and Starr's stomach grumbles, reminding her of its emptiness.

"Nothing," Pierre says and it takes her a little while to realize he answered her question. She searches his eyes and the barely veiled anger there lets her know what she needs to know.

He knows what she did.

She looks away hastily, not ready to deal with his wrath. Not with Mary so close by.

Mary looks over at Starr and smiles.

"Pierre is going to be living with us for a while," she tells Starr.

There is pride in Mary's statement as she reaches for Pierre's hand.

Starr notices the slight hesitates before he returns her hold.

Mary apparently notices too because her smile dims and she asks, "Right, baby?"

Pierre squeezes her hand and beams a smile at her. "That's right, Mary."

Mary returns to the stove with her smile firmly back in place.

She asks Starr, "Isn't that great, Starr?"

"Wonderful," Starr says.

She schools her expression into a warm smile.

"Dinner will be ready soon. Why don't you go freshen up and we can eat."

"Okay, Mom," Starr replies and heads for her bedroom without glancing at Pierre again.

The door closes behind her softly.

No, no, no! This is not how this was supposed to go.

Pierre was supposed to come to her so they can run off and be together.

Her plan seems to have backfired though. It seems to have pushed him further into Mary's arms.

She rushes to find her gun in its hiding place under her bed and grabs her bullets from her purse. She had purchased those separately and had never removed them from there.

She is shaking harder than when she had her near accident. Her eyes burn with unshed tears. Her mind is chaos and her heart is breaking.

She loads her gun as fast as her shaking fingers will allow.

But as soon as the last bullet is loaded, Mary knocks at her door.

"Honey, what's taking you so long? Dinner is ready."

Starr replaces the gun and pushes the turbulent storm of emotions back as she replies, "One more minute and I'll be right there."

"Okay," Mary replies and Starr hears her footsteps fade away.

The interruption calms her mind somewhat.

She gets up and tidies up herself, only them noticing that she had been crying.

A few minutes later she sits at the table and has to endure watching Pierre and Mary act like they are so in love.

She barely eats anything even though she is starving and soon excuses herself with a headache.

After watching television together, Pierre goes off to bed while Mary gathers his clothes and goes into the laundry room to launder them for him.

He only has that one set of clothes and she wants to make sure that it is clean for tomorrow.

She is going to go with him to the mall to get some new outfits in the morning.

She had never thought she and Pierre could have a life together simply because she never thought the day would come when he would leave his wife.

Still, having him show up on her doorstep with that news made her realize how much she *did* want a man of her own. One who had not broken her heart before.

Maybe it is less of a realization that her finally admitting and accepting her desire.

It is time she moved on from Travis and Pierre has offered her the perfect opportunity to do just that.

She does not put on the light, allowing the luminosity from the hallway to guide her.

She loads the washer and puts detergent in. The sound of the water rushing into the appliance fills the space. There is something rather therapeutic about the sound and Mary leans against the white metal for a moment before heading out.

She nearly jumps out of her skin when she realizes that she is not alone.

She makes out the shape of Starr sitting in a darkened corner of the den.

Hand over her chest, she says, "What are doing up, girl?"

It is almost 11:00 PM.

There is a pause before Starr answers, "I can't sleep. I've been wondering about some things."

Still frightened, Mary replies, "Well you scared the shit out of me, Starr."

Even though she cannot make out Starr's features clearly, she can tell her daughter is facing her.

"I am sorry, Mom," Starr says and Mary notices the slow, deliberate way she is talking.

"Are you okay, baby girl? What have you been wondering about?" she asks.

"It's nothing serious," Starr answers.

Mary can tell that she is lying though and persists, "Is it Pierre being here? I know I should have probably discussed it with you first but I really did not think you would a problem with it."

She is determined not to entertain any suspicious about Pierre and Starr anymore. She has already made a fool out of herself at the barbeque for doing that and she does not want to repeat the fiasco. She just wants to forget the whole event happened.

"If you don't want him here, I'll make him leave," she tells her daughter, genuine.

"That is not it, Mom," Starr says, impatience creeping into her voice.

"Did you and your boyfriend have a falling out, then?" Mary continues to question.

Starr sighs. "Something like that. Now can we drop it? I don't want to talk about it. I just want to be alone for a bit."

Mary wants to help but does not know how to so she relents and does what Starr wants.

"Okay, baby girl. But I am here to talk if you need me. No matter what, I love you and you are the most important person in the world to me," she says before heading back to the laundry room.

She might as well fold some clothes that she had lying around while she waits for Pierre's clothes to get done.

It is not like she is likely to fall asleep anytime soon anyway.

One of the listed possible side effects of the medication she is taking is troubling sleep and she is definitely suffering from that malady.

Or maybe it is having a heavy conscious that keeps her up at night.

<hr />

Starr listens to Mary move around in the laundry room.

Her mother has no idea Starr has a gun in her hand and is ready to use right this second at the slightest provocation.

Starr is a woman on the edge and she knows. Thing is, she has no desire to come back from that edge if it gets her wants she needs - her man, Pierre.

She swears that if she listens hard enough, she can hear him breathe.

How can he sleep so soundly with her a few feet away in obvious distress? She thought for sure he would come to her tonight.

Even if he is angry with her, she still wants him around her.

It is around 1:00 AM when Mary enters the darkened den again.

"Honey, I'm going to bed now. You really should get some sleep," Mary advises. "I'm sure a good night's rest will make everything seem much better."

It would be so easy to just get rid of the competition right this second. All I have to do is squeeze the trigger, Starr thinks but says, "Okay, Mom. I am heading in now."

A few minutes later, she falls asleep with a loaded gun underneath her pillow and a heavy heart because of the state of affairs between her and Pierre.

CHAPTER THIRTY

She knows not long Has passed when she feels her bed dip.

Pierre's scent hits her nose and she knows he is here with her. Her heart lights with joy as her eyes fly open.

He has not turned on the light and all she sees is his silhouette.

She reaches for him but his words stop her.

"I'm mad at you. In fact, that does not even cut it. I am livid. You did a very bad thing and now I can go to jail. How are we supposed to be together if I am in prison, Starr? Please explain to me how what you did made any sense? And why were you taping our conversation anyway? Is this what you intended all along? To hurt me like this?"

Tears bubble over the rim of her eyelids.

She had not considered that.

In her mental scenarios, all that was supposed to happen was him coming to her with love and affection. After an initial dose of anger that is.

"I just wanted to break you two up, not cause problems," she says in between sniffles.

"I have no job, no home and no wife now. Are you happy?" he says.

His quiet tone makes her feel all the worse.

She cries harder. She tries to control the loudness of the ragged sounds, not wanting Mary to bust in here. Pierre would not have come if she had not been asleep.

"All I wanted was for us to be together, I swear. To have you to myself," she laments.

"You could have had that but you messed everything up," he accuses in that same steady voice. "Where is the tape, Starr?"

"I can't give it to you," she edges.

She cannot give away the only leverage she has.

He turns toward her then, leaning over her like a huge malevolent shadow.

She is expecting more anger and biting words but instead, he starts kissing on her. He gets into the bed with her and their clothes melt away in the cover of darkness.

They make love quietly with Mary sleeping a few feet away.

The warm, wet and welcoming haven of Starr's body is making Pierre delirious.

And he almost forgets why he came into her bedroom. That is until he spies her cell phone on the dresser next to her bed.

That must be where she has the copies of the tape. Isn't that where all the young people kept everything these days?

He is about to climax bare skinned inside her. He tells her to close her eyes, kissing her lids shut.

He knows that she is putty in his hands when he loves her like this and of course, she does what he says.

He snatches the phone from its location just before he gets release from the pleasure.

As soon as he done, he gets off her and puts his boxers back on. The boxers are the only clothing item available to him right then since he is basically homeless now.

He grinds his teeth in remembered anger at Starr and his fingers tighten around the phone where he is sure to find the evidence of Starr destroying his well put together life.

"I really loved you," he tells her. "I really did."

He is looking down at her.

He has a great view of her since moonlight is streaming in from her bedroom window and pools the bed in light. He knows she cannot see him as well as he rakes a disgusted look over her bare body. Even though he wants to get back in that bed and sex her again, he hates her in that moment. He turns away with a harsh sound coming from the back of his throat, unable to stand the look of her anymore.

She sits up and tries to stop him, calling his name.

He closes her bedroom door softly and goes back into Mary's room with the scent of her daughter still on him.

He will likely disturb Mary if he goes through Starr's phone then so he hides it in his shoes and puts it under the bed.

He climbs into bed and pulls her close before closing his eye.

In the next bedroom, Starr is wide awake.

She is wondering if she has lost Pierre for good and the thought is absolutely devastating.

Eventually, she falls asleep but it is a sleep filled with bad dreams and restlessness.

The next morning she wakes her blurry-eyes and far from rested.

Pierre is the first thing on her mind and she hurriedly freshens up to go into the living room.

The house is empty when she leaves her bedroom.

She patrols the house and realizes how late it is it. The digital clock of the stove reads 11:17 AM.

Suddenly she hears keys at the front door then Mary and Pierre's voice. They are laughing and talking, sounding really chummy.

She remembers that they had planned to go shopping first thing in the morning since Pierre has nothing to wear here.

Starr immediately rushes to the shower. Even though she could not wait to see Pierre a few minutes ago, she cannot bear to see him all lovey dovey with Mary knowing he is mad at her. It is heartbreaking that she might have pushed him closer to Mary.

Still, she cannot find it in herself to regret her actions.

She has gotten one women out of his life. There is only one left.

She stays in the shower for the longest while but eventually she has to leave and face the music.

No one looking in would be able to tell that anything is amiss though. Starr feels no tension in Mary and Pierre' company. He is acting the perfect father figure and Mary is soaking it up. They seem like the textbook little family.

It is grating on Starr's nerves.

Later on that evening, after everyone has run around and done errands for the day, Mary goes to cook dinner and asks Starr to help.

Nerves already shot, Starr snaps, "That's your man, not mine. You cook him dinner."

She can see that Mary gets pissed at her disrespectful comment.

Good, she thinks and goes into her bedroom, slamming the door shut.

She noticed Pierre's raised eyebrow as she passed him but she does not care. She is good and mad at him too now.

Now that she has thought about it, he has no right to be mad at her for what she did. She did what she had to do to get rid of Karen. He should be thankful, not angry with her.

Mary calls her back out when the meal is done and they sit around the table. Pierre and Mary are on one side while Starr is on the other.

Starr is silently fuming as Pierre and Mary carry on their conversation as if nothing happened earlier. She is on the verge of exploding with the anger and unloading on the other two when she feels Pierre brush her legs under the table with his bare foot.

She looks up from where she was glaring daggers at her baked chicken. Their eyes only meet briefly before he turns back to Mary but just the sensation of his touch instantly calms her so that she can think past the madness in her head.

Like a light switches, her mood changes and she smiles. Mary notices and includes her in the conversation she had obviously removed herself from just a few moments earlier.

Pierre continues to touch her under the table and her cheeks flush with the pleasure. She barely holds back a sigh of satisfaction.

Mary's voice pulls her away from her mental bliss when she asks, "Are you okay? You're blushing! Are you thinking about your secret boyfriend?"

Starr answers, "Yes, I am thinking about him."

Her voice practically purrs as she responds because Pierre's advances are being more insistent out of Mary's sight.

Mary shakes her head. Although she is smiling, she looks confused as she continues, "I am glad to see you are happy again but you're so moody all the time. I don't know what has gotten into you."

Starr laughs and replies, "You would not want to know what has gotten *in* to me."

Mary frowns at this statement but Pierre diverts her attention with a question.

Starr smiles for the rest of the dinner, participating when spoken to but otherwise occupied in the dream world where she and Pierre are all alone and making love.

His touch keeps her grounded in that dream.

CHAPTER THIRTY-ONE

After dinner, a mellow Starr offers to do the dishes.

"I'll do it. Go unwind," she tells her mother. "I know you have to get up early for work tomorrow."

"Oh, that is so sweet. Thank you, honey," Mary gushes.

Then Pierre jumps in, "I'll help her. We will get this done faster. Why don't you go have a nice, relaxing bath in the meantime, Mary? That should help you sleep."

"That sounds lovely. Thanks you two."

With that Mary leaves the kitchen and goes down the hall.

A door closes soon after her disappearance.

Pierre and Starr are alone in the room.

They work in silence while they speak glances and small touches at each other as they hear Mary turn on the shower. Every time Pierre gets close to Starr, he touches her in an area that he should not and she loves it.

They are almost done when Mary calls out, "Good night, you two. I'm headed off to bed now."

"Good night," they both call.

The kitchen is spotless a few minutes later and Pierre and Starr look at each other. They are close and the sexual tension between them is almost visible.

They spring apart when there are suddenly footsteps and Mary calls out, "You know what guys? I just cannot seem to fall asleep. This has been the third night in row. Maybe it is that medication I am taking. It probably messed up my sleep cycle."

She appears around the corner in a knee-length nightshirt and hair up in a bonnet.

"Why don't we watch a movie?" Pierre suggests smoothly as if he had not just been about to jump her daughter in the kitchen.

"Oh, that is a great idea," Mary exclaims, excited while Starr tried not to roll her eyes. "That will probably tire me out."

So the three make popcorn then settle down on the couch facing the television.

They are picking a movie when Mary announces, "I'm going to call in sick tomorrow. I am going to take the whole day to spend with my lovely daughter and my new man, my husband to be hopefully."

She giggles and sounds groggy.

Starr does not take her eyes off the television as she clenches her teeth at the last part of Mary's announcement because she just might smack the woman.

"And just catch up on my rest," Mary finishes. "I have been so stressed lately."

Not too stressed to fuck Travis, Starr thinks spitefully.

"Oh, that is nice dear," Pierre says in a placating tone.

Starr injects fake joy into her tone and reinforces, "Yeah, really great, Mom."

Pierre puts in a Blu-ray disk and turns off the lights before settling between the two women to watch the movie.

The intro of the comedy sounds and light begins to flicker from the screen.

The three do not converse anymore but laugh as the funniness unfolds. It does not take long for Mary to start dozing in and out, the effects of her medication and lack of quality sleep the last few nights working on her.

Starr wishes she and Pierre do not have to put up with this act so that they can have time alone and begins to get impatient.

But Pierre puts his hand on her thighs and the feeling dissipates.

Her breath catches in her throat as he runs it up. His hand pushes her skirt higher and higher and higher still.

He does not stop until he cups between her legs with Mary right there next to them. His fingers slip under the fabric of her panties and encounters the stickiness of her wanton desire.

It is scandalous and totally depraved and just right to push Starr's arousal through the roof.

In her mind, she imagines Mary catching them and flipping out. Pierre would shoot her mother down and claim Starr as his one and only woman right then and there.

Her fantasies do not become reality because Mary emits a soft snore.

Pierre maneuvers his hand slowly and carefully as to not rouse Mary but still, he pushes Starr closer and closer to climax. He knows just how to touch her to make her feel right.

Starr is barely containing her sounds of lust. Biting her lip is becoming less and less effective. She is squirming where she sits.

Only the fact that the movie is loud saves them from being given away.

She makes a particularly loud sound. She laughs along with the movie to cover the moan as Mary jumps slightly out of her doze. Pierre laughs too.

Eyes hardly open Mary just follows along and laughs too even though she has no idea what is going on in the movie clearly.

Pierre's slows the pace of his fingers and Starr gets to recover from her breathlessness.

Luckily, Starr's mother dozes right back into unconsciousness seconds after and they can pick up right where they left off.

This time they are not interrupted and Starr reaches the pinnacle. She closes her eyes and has to fight to reign the satisfied sounds in.

She slumps where she sits after. Pierre withdraws his fingers and licks them off. He never once removed his eyes off the movie.

A few minutes later, Starr gets up and goes to her bedroom. She is going to bed.

She does not care what Mary thinks when she gets up. Starr has gotten what she needs for the moments and that is all she cares about.

She and Pierre are playing with fire and she loves it.

The next day, they are all lounging around like Mary wants when the phone rings. Starr is happy this morning and not snapping at her mother while Mary is glad to have a cordial daughter.

Pierre is antsy, given he does not know what is going on with Karen and the cops. He has turned off his cell phone and has not spoken to anyone from his other life since he drove off two nights before.

Is his wife really going to press charges against him?

He does not want to believe that but given the hatred he heard in her voice when they spoke last he is inclined to.

Maybe if I can find a way to just speak to her I can change her mind...

The phone rings again, bringing Pierre away from his thoughts.

Tired of the fake joy being emitted by everyone, Pierre gets up to pick up the phone.

"I'll get it," he says, untangling himself from Mary's grip.

Starr sneaks a grab at his ass as he passes then gets up, saying, "I need a shower."

She goes off in the direction of the bathroom and he watches her rump in the corner of his eye until the door closes behind her.

He picks up the line in the kitchen. "Hello?"

"Who is this?" comes the hostile voice and Pierre immediately knows how the caller is.

Travis.

He chuckles. He loves messing with this man.

"You know exactly who it is," he answers. "What do you want? Calling to check up on *my* girls?"

"What the fuck are doing there? I thought I told you to stay away from my family," Travis snarls. "Let me talk to Starr."

"She is in the shower," he says with an implication in his voice to fuel the other man's anger.

"Well, where the hell is Mary?" Travis demands.

"She's right here. Hold on," Pierre answers smoothly, knowing the man will dig the hold he is already in deeper. All the better for Pierre.

Mary walks over to him and raises an eye in question.

"It's Travis," he tells her and notices the way she immediately becomes frazzled.

He smirks internally. This woman is hopeless at hiding her secret affair with her ex from him.

"Oh! Oh, let me talk to him," she replies with a stammer.

He hands her the phone and leans against the counter next to her. He keeps his eyes her and she squirms under his gaze.

She puts the phone to her ears and greets, "Hi, Travis."

She takes the phone away, looks at it then puts it back at her ear.

"Hello? Hello? There is no answer. He must have hang up. That's so strange," she says and replaces the device.

She gets quiet as Pierre continues to look at her and she looks down. Only the distant sound of the shower running permeates the space.

After a while, she lifts her eyes and says, "What's wrong?"

"Why are you looking like that, Mary?" he replies.

She sighs and seems to come to a decision about something then says, "Pierre, I need to tell you something."

She pauses there and he encourages her to continue by saying, "What is it, Mary? Just tell me."

And just like he knew she would, she confesses to her and Travis sleeping together.

———— ⁘ ————

Starr comes out of the shower to hear Pierre saying, "So, you're cheating on me?"

Mary quickly replies, "It's not what you think. I had not seen you for weeks when this happened. It was only one time too."

Pierre voice is angered as he comes back with, "How could you? After everything I've done for you, this is how you repay me? By taking up with that good for nothing hoodlum?"

Mary clearly does not like his tone because she tells him, "What the hell do you mean after everything you've done for me? I take care of myself. I've never asked you for anything. Anything you've done, you've taken it upon yourself to do. Besides, you're married. How can you tell me I am cheating on you?"

Clutching her towel to her body and still dripping wet, Starr creeps up into the kitchen to see the two arguing. Their body languages are very tense.

Oh, she likes this! Trouble in paradise already…

She almost giggles.

Pierre leans forward aggressively and tells Mary, "You knew that from the start. I did not force you into this relationship. You said you did not care that I have a wife. Are you suddenly changing your mind, Mary? You care about me having a wife *now*? Now that we are not together and you're sleeping with someone else?"

He grabs Mary by the shoulders and shakes her, shouting, "If I never met you, I never would have had all these problems. My life would have never ended up in this mess. This is all your fucking fault."

Mary pushes at his arms and Pierre steps back, clearly taken aback that Mary would respond like that.

Mary gets in his face and in a confused tone, shouts back, "What are you talking about? What problems? You know what? I don't give a damn what you are talking about because you are clearly delusional. How dare you put your hands on me like that? Try that again and you're going to be missing them."

Starr does not like how her mother threatens her man and charges for her bedroom. She is going to get her gun.

CHAPTER THIRTY-TWO

Armed and dangerous, Starr comes back into the kitchen pointing the gun at Mary.

"Don't you dare put your hands on him like that ever again," she shouts.

Both Mary and Pierre turn to her and she takes satisfaction in watching both their eyes round in shock.

"Starr, what are you doing? Have you gone crazy?" Mary yells.

"I have been sleeping with your man," she announces proudly. Finally letting the truth out feels like a weight lifted off her shoulders. "Well, soon to be *my* man once I get you out of the picture."

There is a brief heavy silence as Mary takes this in then she turns to Pierre and says, "Please tell me she's lying. Tell me you have not been sleeping with my child behind my back."

Pierre's smile is sinister as he looks down at Mary. Starr loves the look on his face because she knows that he is going to tell Mary the truth too. Then they can finally be together like she has dreamed about.

"I have been sleeping with Starr since you have been sleeping with her father," he says. "I think that is only fair."

Starr watches the emotions cross Mary's face. Confusion. Hurt. Fury. Realization.

"You bastard!" comes the screech of rage before Mary charges Pierre. She slaps him and the sound of flesh connecting on flesh is even louder.

She continues to hit him while he tries to dodge.

Starr sees red and screams, "Leave my man alone."

She tries to aim the gun at Mary properly but the woman is moving around too much. She does not want to pull the trigger and accidentally hit Pierre instead.

Her scream did have an effect though because Mary stops suddenly and meets Starr's gaze. Starr's hands are shaking and everything is at a standstill.

Maru must have seen the conviction there.

She walks closer to her daughter and says, "What are you doing, sweetheart? This man is not worth it. He is a liar and a cheat. He will never stay in a faithful relationship with you. Look at how he is pitting a mother and daughter against each other, for Pete's sake."

Starr closes the remaining distance between them and shouts in her mother's face. "Shut up. You don't hit my man and you certainly do not speak about him that way. You don't know anything about him, me or our relationship. He *loves* me. He is going to stay with me and be with no one else."

Mary goes not get angry at her announcement like Starr thought she would. Instead, she continues in a gentle tone that grates on Starr's last nerve.

"Baby, you know that I love you. Put the gun down and we can talk about this like civilized, rational adults. There is no need to go this far."

Starr looks over at Pierre and he shakes his head. She moves closer to him, keeping the weapon pointed at her mother.

Mary's eyes fills with tears and she drops to her knees on the floor.

"Why are you doing this? I am your mother," she cries. Her mother looks broken and Starr has only ever seen her like this once before- when Travis let them.

An odd ache blooms in her chest.

"I know," Starr says as Pierre puts an arm around her waist from behind and pulls her close to his body.

She keeps on staring at her mother, conflicted now.

Pierre becomes impatient behind her and yells, "Be done with it already. Get rid of her."

When Starr continues to hesitates, he makes a disgusted sound and shouts louder, "I should have known that you are not woman enough to do it. Give me the fucking gun. I'll do it."

Pierre turns Starr around forcefully then there is a low bang. Mary screams then there is silence.

A look of surprise then horror dawns on Pierre face as he meets Starr's eyes with his.

"You shot me," he said. "You really shot me."

He falls to the floor and Starr stares at him in terrible realization as a dark red shot appears then spreads in the center of his chest.

She had accidentally squeezed the trigger and now there is a hole in Pierre's chest.

She drops the gun, forgetting it immediately, and drops to her knees at his side.

His eyes are hateful as they look up at Starr. "Damn, I should have never fucked you. My life is definitely fucked now."

Red liquid pours out of the side of his mouth as he struggles to get the words.

"I did not mean to," she says quietly. She puts her hand over the wound and it gets soaked in blood instantly. Beneath her touch his chest his moving up and down rapidly and he is gasping.

"Fuck," he breathes and it is his last breath.

The light fades from his eyes and that quick the man that she would die for is dead. His chest stops moving under her hand.

She begins to cry then feels Mary come up behind her and embrace her.

She does not fight the touch even though it makes her skin crawl. She cannot move, shocked that Pierre is gone.

"It's okay, baby," Mary is saying over and over again but Starr doubts it will ever be again.

They are both bawling their eyes out when the door suddenly bursts in.

Travis and Pierre's wife rush in. Behind them, police fan into the house.

In a daze, Starr watches all the activity around as if is happening from a distance. She is hauled out of a protesting Mary's grip and taken out of the house by the authorities.

She does not fight. She does not care anymore. All she had to live for is lying on the floor of her mother's house, take away from her.

———— ⚭ ————

Travis grabs Mary and tries to restrain her as the police take Starr away. She is escorted out of the house in nothing more than towel and crazed look on her face, and placed in the back of a cruiser. They soon take her away and he vows to get her the best attorney he can.

He knew something was going on. He *knew* it. He just wishes his daughter did not have to be the one to pay in the end.

As far as he is concerned Pierre gets off easy because he would have beat the shit out of him if he had the chance.

He sees Karen walk out of the house, escorted by a uniformed police officer. Her eyes are dry despite the fact that her husband lays dead a few feet away.

He had dug as far as he could in this Pierre character, going so far as to hire a PI. The man had found out quite a bit in the last few hours including the fact that he had a wife and kid tucked away on the other side of town.

Travis had approached Karen and found out about Pierre's involvement in her unborn baby's murder. She had pressed charges against him and he was on the run from police.

He had called Mary from her house, hoping to warn her but Pierre had answered instead.

He had informed Karen and the two had raced over here with the police on their tail.

They had pulled up in front of the house just as a gunshot had sounded. Nothing could have shocked him more than seeing a dead Pierre on the kitchen floor.

A crowd has gathered outside of Mary's house. People are screaming, crying and hollering and he can hear the murmurs as he tries to comfort a hysterical Mary.

"How did it come to this?" someone asks.

He does not understand himself.

Mary suddenly holds onto him really tight and makes eye contact.

Her eyes are red and swollen from crying.

"I am so sorry that I did not listen to you. This is all my fault. I could have stopped it all if I had just listened," she cries in between hiccups and sobs.

He cups her cheeks and his heart breaks seeing her like this. She should not have to hurt like this.

"Don't do that, baby. Don't blame yourself. This all falls on that scumbag."

Mary just sobs harder at his words and he drags her closer, enfolding her in his arms.

One And A Half Years Later

Months of court proceedings led to this day.

Starr is led into the courtroom by a bulky female police officer and placed before the judge. She is dressed in a white shirt and black pants with her hair pulled back into a tight bun. Her face is bare and she looks years passed her age, so far removed from the carefree young lady who just graduated high school.

The man wears a severe look as the attorneys verbally battle one last time for her freedom. She is still and her face wear no emotions. She does not even look back her mother and father who sit only two rows behind her.

Karen sits all the way in the back, stone-faced.

There is silence three hours later as the older man gives the jury's decision.

"You, Starr Dixon are hereby accused of second-degree murder."

Mary breaks down into terrible sobs while Travis holds onto her once more.

Their daughter is led away a few minutes later. The time that she will spend in prison will be handed down later.

Still, Starr remains emotionless and does not glance at her distraught parents.

EPILOGUE

Three years have passed since Starr was sentenced to twenty-five years in prison.

It is a bright and sunny autumn afternoon and Mary and Travis are in the neighborhood kid's park playing with an almost four-year-old Hope Starr Dixon. Other kids and their guardians are running around and having fun too.

Mary watches on as Travis pushes Hope on the swing. The little girl looks so much like her mother as she laughs in enjoy and excitement, screaming, "Higher, Daddy. Push me higher!"

Hope is Starr's and Pierre's biological daughter but she calls Mary and Travis Mummy and Daddy. She has no relationship with her half-sister sired in Pierre's marriage because Karen wants nothing to do with them. Maybe one day that will change. Mary hopes so.

Starr had had no idea that she had been pregnant when she had been arrested. She had given birth before her sentence and Mary had vowed to take care of the baby long before she had seen her. She had fallen in love with the innocent infant on first sight and has never regretted raising her as her own. She had been squirming and fussy when the authorities had brought Hope to Mary. But as soon as Mary had lifted her out of the arms of the government worker, the baby had settled down and cooed for her grandmother.

Hope has no idea that her real mom is incarcerated. She and Travis had told Hope that her birth mother is unwell and someplace where she can get better. In the loving, innocent way of children her age, Hope had said, "I can't wait until I meet her. I hope she feels better soon."

And Mary hopes the same.

She visited Starr earlier today and had gotten the response she always does.

Starr had refused to see her. Starr claims to have been absolutely in love with Pierre for years, as well as he with her, and thinks that Mary kept them from being together. She listens to no reason and is firm in her belief no matter what anyone else tells her.

Mary's daughter somehow blames her for Pierre's death and has not forgiven her despite all the years that have passed and all of Mary's attempts to reconcile.

Starr's blame only adds to the guilt that Mary feels.

She should have never started an affair with a married man, far less brought him around her under aged daughter.

But what she blames herself for most is not heeding the warning signs that she had seen and chosen to ignore. Even without Travis's warnings, her intuition had told her something was off and she had not listened to it.

For that, she would carry the shame to her grave.

Still, she tries not to let Starr's continued rejection or her responsibility in the tragedy that occurred weigh her down. She has cried over it long and hard. Now, she tries to concentrates on the positive.

She is determined to focus on the goodness in her life right now. She has gotten a second chance at motherhood and is determined to get it right this time.

Travis laughs at something the little girl says, pulling Mary's attention to him.

She married him again.

He has been her rock these past few years. She honestly does not know what she would have done if he had not been around. She fell in love with him all over again.

They have built a good life together. He has recently opened up his own motorcycle repair shop while she has gone back to school to pursue a career in nursing. She sold the house she used to live in and they bought a house closer to the city. She did not need the constant reminders of what happened by staying in the old neighborhood.

Besides, it would not be healthy for Hope. If they had stayed, she was bound to hear rumors about her mother and her father's untimely death.

Travis looks up as Hope takes off running toward the seesaw and smiles at her. She pushes her troubles to the back of her mind and smiles back with the same love and affection he is beaming at her.

"Come play with us," he beckons.

She gets up and goes to join her family.

Maybe one day the last member of their family would be able to join them with a heart full of love equal to theirs.

THE END

Printed in the United States
by Baker & Taylor Publisher Services